THE BACHELOR DINNER

THE BACHELOR DINNER

BY

OLIVE M. BRIGGS

AUTHOR OF "THE BLACK CROSS," "THE FIR AND THE PALM"

*"Le plus grand malheur de la vérité est
d'être invraisemblable"*

CHARLES SCRIBNER'S SONS

NEW YORK::::::::::::::::::::::::1912

TO MY CHUM-BROTHER

A. T. B.

IN MEMORY OF OUR EARLY COMRADESHIP

CONTENTS

ILLUSTRATIONS

THE BACHELOR DINNER

The Bachelor Dinner

IT was an accidental sort of an affair, that dinner: the guests drawn from all quarters of the
globe, travellers most of them, mere strangers,
who met only to part again; the invitations given
out at the last moment, haphazard as it were.
But of all that group of men present there is not
one, I venture to say, who will ever forget it; not
one, but to whom the very mention of Paris recalls
the memories of that extraordinary night.

On the morning before—it all comes back to
me as if it were yesterday—I had locked the door
of my studio behind me, and was just starting
down the Rue Bonaparte with Barry Whittemore.
We were sauntering along with arms linked, smoking, absorbed in some argument or other as usual;
and had barely gone ten yards when he stopped all
of a sudden. I felt his arm give a jump under
mine, and he turned white as chalk.

"By Jove, McD.," he said, "if that isn't Travis!"

"Who? . . . Where?"

"Dan Travis! Dan Travis here in Paris! Of all
things! You haven't forgotten the snake dance,
have you?"

The Bachelor Dinner

I gave an exclamation and we both darted forward.

The man whom we thus intercepted was standing with his back toward us, gazing down into the window of an old-print shop. When he heard his name called, he wheeled about like a flash and stared at us blankly.

"Don't you know me, Travis?"

Barry's hand-shake was warm and was as warmly returned, but again I noticed that curious whiteness go over his face, a pallor that was almost instantly reflected on the bronze skin of the other.

"You! . . . You, Whittemore!"

Travis still stood staring as if turned into stone.

In the moment of awkward silence that followed, each seemed to be undergoing a desperate struggle to regain self-control, to readjust a mask that had slipped.

Barry broke in with a nervous laugh.

"I'd have recognized those shoulders of yours anywhere, old man. We've had to follow them too often on the foot-ball field to forget them now—eh, McD.?"

"Not in a thousand years!" I cried. "How are you, Captain?"

Travis roused with a start.

"McD.!" he said slowly. "To be sure! . . .

The Bachelor Dinner

You were left tackle on the 'Varsity, weren't you?
Of course, I remember now. Or was it end?"
He passed his hand over his forehead several times,
as if to brush away the recollections of the years in
between. "The last time I saw you——"

Barry and I both burst into laughter.

"McD. was dancing the snake dance with the
crowd around the goal-posts, and you, Travis,
were being borne aloft on the shoulders of the team.
All of us yelling, screaming, hurrahing like a pack
of wild Indians. Great Scott, what a game that
was! You led Yale to victory that time, Captain, and none of the boys will ever forget it."

Barry's manner was enthusiastic, almost boister-
ous in its endeavor to appear natural. Travis
turned to me quickly.

"You must forgive me for not having known
you at once," he exclaimed, "but you've got a mustache since the old days, McD., and are certainly
stouter. What the deuce are you doing in Paris?"

It was the same winning way, the smile that had
endeared him to his college mates, and had made
him their leader from the very beginning. He had
that faculty with men, a born supremacy that was
never questioned. His steady eyes looked down
into mine.

"I'm in residence here, Captain. I've set up
a studio."

The Bachelor Dinner

"The dickens you have!" Travis laid his hand on my shoulder. "You a painter, McD.? Well, I'm glad to hear it. I'm jolly glad to hear that. You always were a talented chap!... Whereabouts?"

"This very street. Just above, not far from the Beaux Arts. Come back with us, will you?"

"Why, you're right in the rear of my quarters, then! I'm on the St. Benoit, just behind. You must overlook my garden.... No! Thanks, McD., thanks awfully, but I have a business appointment. I've got to be off."

"What!" I cried. "You don't mean to tell me we're neighbors here, and never knew it!... Hold on a moment, Travis. What's your hurry?"

Barry had drawn back.

Travis gave him a strange glance and hesitated.

"No, really, McD., much obliged. I'm late as it is."

He took out his watch, snapping the lid back in a nervous, jerky, rather absent-minded way. "Yes, yes, it's past the hour now. By the way—" Travis put the watch back into his pocket. "You couldn't come to dinner with me to-night, both of you—could you? A few men are running in, interesting fellows you might like to meet. Quite informal."

I looked at Barry.

6

The Bachelor Dinner

He had turned away, and was studying the prints in the window with the air of one who sees them for the first time. I could tell from his absorption that he had heard.

"Well, I don't know—" I began rather helplessly. The situation was certainly peculiar between those two. "I rather hate to get into evening clothes! . . . Any women, Travis?"

This was to gain time more than anything else.

"No," he said shortly. "Come as you are."

Barry bent a little lower over one of the engravings. It was a perfectly worthless one, as any one could have told at a glance.

"Go, McD.," he called back carelessly over his shoulder. "That engagement of ours doesn't matter in the least. Don't mind me. I'll go to the Châtelet."

"I asked you both," said Travis.

A sudden swift look passed between the two men, one whose meaning it was impossible to fathom. Pride, concern, bitterness, appeal—a strong emotion, compelling, overmastering—the secret of some memory shared! It was all there, bared for an instant, as a dark valley in the flash of a searchlight. I stood staring from one to the other, dumbfounded, startled out of all self-possession.

The look was a short one, but it spoke volumes.

The Bachelor Dinner

"I'll come!" exclaimed Barry. "I'll come, Dan! . . . Good-by, old chap."

Travis never opened his mouth. He gave his hand to Barry with a hasty clasp, nodded to me. In a second more he was striding off, around the corner and out of sight.

Barry and I walked on together. For a block or more there was dead silence.

"Nice, warm spring day, isn't it?" said Barry after a while, in an off-hand way.

"Funny thing that!"

"What?"

"Haven't you ever noticed that big studio window in the rear, the one with yellow curtains and a statue of the Niké in the centre? There's clematis growing all over the blinds."

"Oh, yes! I've noticed it."

"Well, that must be his."

"Whose?" said Barry. "Do you know, McD., I think Paris in the early spring is a sight for the gods! Suppose we go out to the Bois this afternoon."

"What's he doing here in Paris, I wonder."

Barry yawned.

"Not an artist, is he?"

"How in the world should I know, McD.? I haven't followed the careers of all the fellows any more than you have! . . . Here's the brasserie."

The Bachelor Dinner

He flung himself down by one of the little tables that were strewn along the pavement, and I followed suit.

"Deux cafés au lait! Vite!" he said irritably to the waiter. "Allez, be off!... Warm, isn't it, McD.?"

"Hm-m, so-so. Strange, the way things come back to one!" I bit the end off my cigar meditatively. "Now I hadn't thought of that foot-ball game in years. We expected the Captain to set the North River on fire in those days; didn't we, Whittemore? Handsome, dare-devil chap he was! Well, he may have for all I know. You remember I left college before the term closed. You haven't seen him since, I suppose?"

"Since?... Since what?"

"The game."

"Travis, you mean?... Yes, I saw him at Commencement. Got a match anywhere about you, McD.? I hate these confounded foreign things that fizzle."

I held my lighted cigar out toward him; and as he bent to ignite his own, our faces almost met for a moment.

"Good Lord, Barry! What's up? What the devil is the matter with you? Do you think I'm blind, not to see that you've been in a blue funk ever since you first laid eyes on that fellow? If

9

he affects you that way, we won't go to his plagued dinner; we'll send him a note."

"No, no," said Barry; "you don't understand. If you knew— Well, I'll tell you, McD.; I might as well. I'll tell you the whole story. You've been an intimate friend of mine for years. We've been pretty close, haven't we? . . . But, first, swear by everything that is holy——"

"Of course, old man!"

"Whatever I say to you now will never cross your lips under any circumstances?"

"Never, Whittemore— never! You ought to be able to trust me by this time."

"Very well then," said Barry. He gave a hasty glance over his shoulder. Our order lay already served on the table. The waiter had gone; there was no one about. He took up his cigar and stared straight ahead of him. I poured out the coffee for us both without speaking.

"Good, is it?"

"Oh, pretty fair."

"McD., I don't know how to begin! . . . Tell me, you always liked Travis, didn't you? You always admired him?"

"All the fellows did."

"Well, his being captain of the foot-ball team made him popular naturally; but apart from that?"

"Apart from that! Why, Dan Travis would

have been just as popular if he'd never kicked a ball. You know that, Whittemore, as well as I do."

"How do you explain it?"

"You can't explain those things."

Barry knocked the ash from his cigar and looked up. "What I'm trying to get at, McD., is this. You saw him just now, for the first time since the game. Did you think him much changed?"

"Yes, I did."

"In what way?"

"Of course everyone changes more or less in ten years. You've changed yourself, Barry; so have I. I've a mustache, and a picture or two in the Salon, to say nothing of avoirdupois; and you've won, heaven knows how many cases, and are a rising light at the bar. Now, Travis—" My eyes met Barry's suddenly, and I saw that he was watching me with a curious intentness. "Well, when I went down to Cuba that time, Whittemore—you remember when I left college— our regiment came in for some hard fighting. I was laid up in hospital almost directly myself, but I happened to see the poor chaps who were left, just after one of the worst engagements. I saw them as they came limping back, their flags bedraggled and bullet-ridden. They were strong men and brave men, they had faced death gallantly, and they looked as if they had gone through hell. I thought of this when I saw Travis."

Barry's hand reached out for his cup. It was shaking so that the coffee spilled over.

"You never knew, did you, McD.," he said suddenly, "that Travis and I once spent a fortnight together in camp up in Canada? It was the year you came abroad."

"Upward of five years that would be then."

"Five years ago this summer exactly. You were asking whether Dan and I had met one another since the foot-ball game, since graduation. My God, yes—we met! I wish to heaven we never had. And yet there wasn't a fellow in college thought more of Travis than I did, as you know."

Barry took a swallow or two of the coffee and set the cup carefully back on the table. "Than I do now, for the matter of that, although I judged him harshly enough at the time; too harshly, McD., by far. I felt that afterward. But I was young then and inexperienced. Five years of law practice teaches a man a thing or two about life. By Jove! Human nature, I can tell you, as revealed through the secrecy of a lawyer's office, is a strange and wonderful thing."

"Pretty low down, I take it."

"No," he said, "no, McD., you're mistaken

The Bachelor Dinner

there. On the surface perhaps, yes; but underneath, when the real bottommost depths are stirred, there may be a god in every devil." Barry stopped and drew a long whiff from his cigar.

"Well, our camp was right in the heart of the forest. You know how those Canadian camps are. An opening in the timber where the trees had been hacked away; the cabin built of the rough logs; one large room for lounging and eating, with verandas almost as wide again; and then the sleeping-tents. The lake, a splendid sheet of water, stretching out for miles in the distance, dotted with innumerable islands—hundreds of them, McD., literally thousands! It was that that made it so terrible in the end—such a nightmare. We could never know, we could never be sure——" He breathed heavily, caught himself up, and smoked on for a little without speaking.

"There were about twenty of us in all, mostly men, but a few women. Travis was there with his wife."

"His what?"

"You didn't know he was married, McD.? Well, he was, more's the pity. A man of that sort never ought to get married. No. It's like one of those bucking cow-boy broncos. Free, under the saddle, they go all right; but touch them with harness and they kick it to bits."

13

The Bachelor Dinner

"Bosh, Whittemore! Have another cup of coffee? . . . Why can't you just say in plain English he married the wrong woman and be done with it? Unless I'm very much mistaken——"

"You are mistaken."

"A man— Hold on, Barry, let me finish! . . . A man like Travis, I say, with those eyes of his, and that mouth! You mean to tell me that if he loved a woman——"

"He loved her, McD.! Heaven knows he loved her! There was never any doubt about that in my mind from the first moment the thing happened. Perhaps if we had never questioned it— But the whole affair was so strange, so unaccountable; it all came so suddenly. When I think of those awful two weeks, what we had to go through, it makes me shudder!" Barry was silent for a moment or two, turning his face away from the light.

"Everything was pleasant enough at the start. You know how it is in those camps, McD., when the men are good fellows, jolly, up to all kinds of pranks, and the women fit in. It was all right until Miss Mallory came. She was a cousin of Dan's. One of those innocent-eyed, fluffy-haired, Keats-and-Shelley-under-a-tree sort of women. A regular little cat. But she took all the men; she took like wildfire! That was at the bottom of the whole

14

mischief, I think now, as far as Travis was concerned. He didn't really care a row of pins for the girl, but she was his cousin, they'd been all but engaged once (so the story got about anyway), and the fact is, Dan never could stand being cut out. He always had to be first at everything. Don't you remember—just as in the foot-ball days? Whatever he did, he was always captain!"

"What sort of a woman was his wife, Barry?"

"His wife?"

Barry took his cigar out of his mouth and shook off the ashes.

"I don't know," he said. "She wasn't exactly beautiful, if that's what you mean. She was a little bit of a dark gypsy-like thing, with short, curly black hair (cut off after a fever or something), and she used to go about in a red sweater, with one of Dan's caps on the back of her head, as gay and natural and happy-hearted as a boy. You'd have liked to paint her, McD. She was very young, and when she stood up beside Travis's great bulk in her short skirt, she looked a mere child. She adored him."

"And he?"

"Travis? . . . Well, at first, he barely let her out of his sight. They were always together. It was all right, I tell you, until that cat came; and then,

The Bachelor Dinner

almost immediately, we noticed the change. If she'd been older, more experienced, more like other women, I suppose she would have stood out for her rights, and gotten them too; but she wasn't that sort. She drew back instead; apparently paid no attention to anything, and gave the other woman the field."

"The worst thing she could have done with a fellow like Travis!"

"Exactly. Nobody saw it then; but the whole thing is as plain as a pike-staff now. Her indifference must have acted as a goad on Dan, and maddened him simply beyond endurance. It all began carelessly enough in the beginning. Then, when it dawned on him she didn't care, he evidently swore to himself he'd make her."

"Interesting situation, that!"

"Interesting, so long as the gun hangs fire. If those two had been just the commonplace, ordinary married couple, the trouble would undoubtedly have soon blown over and nothing would have happened. The difficulty was that they were not. Both were proud, high-tempered, passionate natures, reckless to the extreme; caring desperately and afraid to show it. If only we had let them alone, McD.! My God, I've said it to myself a thousand times since. If only we had had the sense to leave them alone! That is

The Bachelor Dinner

where I blame myself, and shall to my dying day. Although as heaven is my witness, what I did was done out of no disloyalty to him—Dan knows it now—but simply and solely to make things a little easier for her, and to bring him back to his senses if possible. I thought—we all thought—if she could only manage to work on his jealousy, it would all come right. And so like a blind fool I played the game; she, poor child, falling in with it in her misery; outwardly gay, laughing, full of fun, the life of the camp, as heedless of Travis and his love-makings as if they had never existed. Inwardly, no one will ever know what she suffered, what she must have suffered before——"

Barry's voice grew husky, and again he turned his head, the smoke from his cigar curling up in little rings, floating slowly in wreaths and melting away.

"As I tell you, McD., an outsider, not knowing the relationship, would never have dreamed that anything was wrong. But the camp knew, and the camp talked; not openly, of course, but in groups and in whispers, under their breath. So the storm was brewing. The more I devoted myself to Nita, the more the other men tried to lure Miss Mallory away, the worse Travis got. The reason, of course, is clear enough now, but we couldn't make head or tail of it then. Some of

17

The Bachelor Dinner

us were pretty strong in our condemnation of Dan, but nobody dared to make any remonstrance. Travis isn't the kind of man one would venture to take such a liberty with!

Meanwhile there wasn't a soul in the camp who didn't feel admiration for Nita. Every day her eyes grew bigger, the shadows under them deeper, her cheeks more flushed. Every day Travis and Miss Mallory would stay out in the forest a little longer. When they came back, the boat would be gone and we two with it; the red sweater only a blot in the distance. Dan could hear his wife's laugh ringing over the water. While I fished, she would handle the rudder and watch. Whenever she laughed I knew that she saw them. The heart-break behind that laugh of hers was apparent to every one but Travis. It was all the rest of us could do to listen and look on in silence. Yet to him, there was a sting in the mere careless sound of it that seemed to rouse the very devil! Looking back on that time, McD., the wonder is that he didn't kill me. I'm sure we all wanted to pummel him for being such a blind, besotted idiot, to be wasting his time with that fluffy creature, while the look on that little wife's face— Bah!"

Barry's voice broke. "I can't bear to think of it, McD.; I can't bear to think of it! All the while the fault was partly my own. If I had had

The Bachelor Dinner

the slightest notion of the way matters stood between them, if I had guessed for an instant! Great heavens! . . . Afterward, of course, I took all the blame on myself that I could. Who wouldn't have in the terrible days that followed! But Dan never would hear of it. He shut me right up from the very beginning; shouldered the responsibility with his face drawn and his teeth set. The first night we thought he would go insane! The suddenness of it all was like a blow between the eyes. He was stunned, dazed. But after that, the man never flinched mentally or physically, not for a second. He went through his hell like a god and a hero, and the scars are there to-day in his face. You saw them, McD.?"

"Yes, I saw them, Barry."

"When his eyes fell on me just now, you know, he could scarcely bear it! The thing came back to us both in a flash. You saw that too?"

"Yes, I saw that too."

Barry moved uneasily on the hard iron chair. and pushed the crockery back with his fingers.

"Look out, old man, you'll smash something!"

"Yes, yes! . . . Well, the crash came, McD., and it fell in this way. Whether Nita had overheard some of the gossip, or just what happened, we never knew; but one evening we had finished supper and were all gathered about the log fire in the

The Bachelor Dinner

cabin. It was one of those September nights when it is starlight, you know, but a little frosty and damp after sundown, and we were glad enough to stay indoors for a change. Well, the talk got around to divorce, of all subjects; and as ill luck would have it, the matter happened to be introduced by Travis. Something he had been reading in the newspaper started him.

'Hello,' he cried, 'did you see this? Westerman wants to get a divorce, and his wife won't let him!'

'Westerman, the artist?' somebody exclaimed. 'Why, he's only been married a year or two! What does he want to get a divorce for?'

'To marry another woman, I suppose,' said Travis.

Nita had drawn back into the shadow of the room, but in the play of the firelight I thought she was shivering.

'How about that, Barry? What's the law? Can she prevent him from doing as he chooses in the matter?'

'Of course she can, Travis.'

I answered roughly and tried to turn the subject, but Dan by some strange fatality persisted.

'How, Barry?'

'If she is innocent! What do you think? The man can't force her to give him his freedom.'

The Bachelor Dinner

'Pretty rough on a fellow that, if he's tired of a woman and wants to leave her!'

A sudden silence fell on the room, McD., when he said this. There wasn't a sound but the fire crackling. You know that strange, eerie, electric feeling that comes over a little gathering of people sometimes, like the tenseness of atmosphere that precedes thunder? Dan lit his pipe.

'Yes, I tell you, if I were in Westerman's shoes, I'd be shot if any woman could hold me!'

A log broke on the fire and fell, scattering a shower of sparks against the fender. There was silence again.

'It wouldn't do the husband any good, even if the wife did get a divorce; would it, Mr. Whittemore?' Miss Mallory looked up from her lap, where she had been folding and unfolding her plump white hands. She drawled slightly and her voice carried. 'He couldn't marry again in any case, could he, as long as she lived?'

Really, McD., the girl didn't mean any harm by it. It was just one of those stupid, senseless things that ought never to have been spoken. She was vain, addle-headed, but not vicious.

'By Jove!' said Travis, 'I believe that's so! Suppose we go out on the lake a while, Molly?'

He sprang to his feet, and Miss Mallory also. It was then that I noticed that Nita had vanished.

The Bachelor Dinner

Travis evidently noticed it too. He gave an uneasy glance around and stood undecided. For a moment I thought the plan was abandoned.

'Aren't you going, Dan?'

Miss Mallory was winding one of those pink woolly things around her head as she said this, and gave him a coquettish look. Travis stared past her as if he had not heard. Then he frowned and hesitated.

'Wait a moment! Yes! I'll be back directly!' and he dashed out, slamming the door behind him.

Whether it was premonition, or what it was, I don't know, McD., but we all sat there as if turned into statues. Miss Mallory waited; we all waited. Not one word was spoken. It was strange, ghastly! What were we waiting for? After the door slammed, there was the sound of his footsteps outside, then his voice hallooing. A long silence, and then rapid footsteps returning. When Dan flung back the door he was as white as a sheet.

'She isn't in the tent, and the boat's gone!' he panted. 'Is Barry around?'

'We're all here,' I cried. 'By heaven, Travis, you haven't let her go out alone?'

There was more of accusation in my tone than I'd intended, but by that time we were all overwrought and excited. For a second I thought he was going to strike me. Then he wheeled like a

The Bachelor Dinner

flash and called out to the others: 'There's another boat! One of you fellows come with me, will you?' He was off again, running.

It is still a mystery to me, McD., it always has been, why we were all so suddenly frightened. The night seemed to grow black all at once; the stars disappeared. A damp mist began to creep over the lake. We shivered and drew closer to one another instinctively, dreading the shadows. The door of the cabin stood wide open. The fire burned, and the great logs crackled cheeringly, invitingly; but no one went back.

In another hour every boat had been borrowed from a neighboring camp, and the men were all out scouring the water. It got to be midnight. The mist had pretty well closed in by then. Still no sign of Nita; no sign of Travis or his companion. It was as if the fog bank had opened and swallowed them up. In the early dawn the boats began to drift back, one by one.

Not to my dying day, McD., shall I ever forget that scene. How ghastly it was, you could never imagine, unless you'd been through it! Those huddled watching women on the bank, their trembling hands reaching out for the boat prows. The searchers landing disheartened, exhausted. The question—and then that terrible answer.

'Any trace yet?'

The Bachelor Dinner

'Not yet! . . . Nothing!'"

Barry sprang up from his chair all at once, and took two or three rapid turns back and forth by the tables. There were little beads of sweat on his forehead.

"The sun was rising, all the boats were in; and then at last, at last—Travis! When we saw him we knew at a glance what had happened. They had found the boat floating bottom upward."

"Had a wind sprung up, Barry?"

"No."

"Then, what had upset it?"

"Why, you know those Canadian canoes, McD., they're like egg-shells. Any sudden move would be enough."

"With a novice, yes; but was she a novice?"

Barry put up his hand and stopped me.

"That was the dreadful part of it, McD., the inexplicable part! Nita was one of the best canoeists you ever saw, absolutely at home on the water. Travis had taught her to swim himself; and the lake that night was as still as a mill-pond. There was only the one thing to think, of course. Either that or she had swum to one of the islands. Travis believed the latter himself. Nothing would shake him. So of course we started to work on that theory. Island after island, island after island! To examine each single one was impossible,

24

The Bachelor Dinner

but the search was kept up all day and all night. Rockets were fired, signals were flared. We all did our best. The grit and endurance of Travis was marvellous. For a week or more I doubt if he slept."

"Was the body found?"

"No, strangely enough, it wasn't. I suppose that is why he kept up his hope. To the very end, poor fellow, he expected to find her, waiting and watching for him on one of those islands! He loved her, McD. No one who lived through those days with him could doubt it."

"What became of the other woman?"

"Miss Mallory? I haven't the faintest notion. What generally becomes of the speck of dust that clogs the wheels and brings on the catastrophe? It disappears somehow! . . . Well, the days went by and the camp broke up. One by one the men went home, until finally only Travis and I were left. When the snow began to fall and the lake froze over—my practice was going to pieces, McD., what else could I do? My mother was dependent on me. I had to leave him."

"You don't mean to tell me, Whittemore, that Dan stayed up there alone all winter?"

Barry nodded. "I remonstrated with him, we all did; but it was useless. 'You don't know what it is!' he would say. 'Every night in my sleep

The Bachelor Dinner

I hear her voice, calling to me, crying my name!'
Every night he used to get up and go out on the
lake and search. If he didn't, he said, the thought
of her out alone in the dark and the cold would
have driven him mad."

"Was that the last you saw of him, Barry?"

Barry smoked on for a moment in silence. He
was still on his feet, moving restlessly in and out
among the tables. Several times the waiter had
appeared in the doorway; and then, receiving no
sign, had vanished.

"Until to-day, McD. We wrote to him, of
course, every one of us, over and over again, but
Dan never answered. And from that time to
this, five long years now, for all I knew he might
have been dead! . . . Have you finished your
coffee?"

"Just a second, Barry. The body was never
found, you say?"

"No, but it happens that way sometimes. Of
course it may have turned up in the spring; but
I doubt it. We never heard anything."

"You always felt perfectly sure?" I asked.

He took up his hat. "Oh, there were rumors,
all sorts of tales, wild notions—if that's what you
mean. But I never put any faith in them, nor
did Travis. That talk on divorce was the last
straw, poor little girl! She was broken-hearted;

and she died that Dan might be free to marry the woman she thought he loved. It was perfectly clear."

Barry's voice was husky. "I wouldn't have told you the story, McD., if it hadn't been for the dinner to-night—to avoid embarrassment in case you had asked the natural questions, not knowing about it. You saw he was sensitive; you'll have to be careful. Don't let him imagine, of course, for an instant——"

"Of course not!" I interrupted. "But, by the way, has it ever occurred to you that Travis may have married again, Barry?"

"Never!" he cried. "Never, McD.! . . . Why, didn't you hear? It's a Bachelor Dinner."

Fortesquieu's Wife

THE clock in the court-yard was just striking seven, when Barry Whittemore and I began climbing the narrow, steep stairs that led up through the darkness to Travis' apartment. Except for a faint glimmer of gas on the landings, the well of the stairway was lost in shadow. We felt our way cautiously.

"Quatrième, was it, McD.?"

"Quatrième, yes. So the concierge said; but, confound it, I don't know how high up we are! I've lost count—have you?"

"Strike a match, then," said Barry. "Hold on, McD., give a look at this card. Isn't that his?"

We both bent our heads. I held the match in my hand, peering.

"For the life of me, Barry, I can't make it out. Yes! . . . No, wait a moment!"

"It's abominable the way they light these places!" exclaimed Whittemore angrily; "dangerous too!" He muttered something under his breath and struck another match. We both peered closer.

The name on the card was: *J. Fortesquieu.*

Fortesquieu's Wife

All of a sudden the door before which we were stooping swung back, and in the opening stood Travis.

"I thought I heard talking out here," he said. "You had trouble finding me? Yes, I was afraid so!... Come in, come in!"

For a moment he stood there framed in the light: a commanding figure, his shoulders broad, his dark head thrown back, his hands both out with a gesture of welcome. He was smoking a pipe, and his coat was a black velvet smoking-jacket, which he wore like a tuxedo, with a white tie and shirt-front. In spite of certain lines in his face, a faint powdering of gray in the thick dark hair falling over his temples, that tense look about the mouth as of one who has lived, whose youth is behind him, I noticed at once that he was strikingly handsome.

"Come in!" Dan repeated.

The door shut behind us, and we followed him into the dimly lit studio.

It was a large space, lofty, curiously shaped. At one end was the high glass studio window, the upper panes screened by long yellow curtains, the lower left open. Beyond was the garden. Just before the window, on a pedestal, stood the Niké, a beautiful cast in terra cotta. All about the walls were paintings hung, and books, shelf after shelf, running up to the ceiling. In one corner

The Bachelor Dinner

was a short spiral staircase, such as one often sees in libraries. It led to a gallery. At the end of the gallery was a door. Both the gallery and the staircase itself were of wood, blackened by age and exquisitely carven. Strewn over the floor were rugs here and there, costly, oriental in coloring. In the centre of the room stood a round table. It was covered with damask, set with silver, lighted with curiously wrought candelabra. There were eight places.

Except for the candles that flickered in the breeze, the only light was the dusk from the garden. Several men were lounging about in the shadows, smoking and chatting. They rose as we entered. Travis took his pipe out of his mouth and laid a hand on each of our shoulders.

"Gentlemen," he said, "my college mates, Mr. McD., Mr. Whittemore—my friends, General Chatterton, Signore Taglioni, Count Nicot, and Mr. DeJong. . . . Help yourself, Barry!"

He motioned to half a dozen boxes of cigars and cigarettes that lay open on the table, and then flung himself back in an easy-chair from which he had evidently just risen.

"Ménard is going to be late," he said carelessly. "He's just in the midst of a new experiment; did you know that, Nicot? We'll wait a bit anyway! Suppose you go on with your story, DeJong."

Fortesquieu's Wife

As my eyes grew accustomed to the half light, I could make out the faces faintly at first, then more and more distinctly. The Count was slim and small and dark, very foreign looking, with a short mustache which he twirled incessantly. DeJong was big and blond, with a hearty laugh and honest blue eyes. His skin was ruddy and bronzed like a sailor. As Travis spoke, he was engaged in stuffing his pipe with tobacco. He wedged it well in with his thumb before answering.

"You mean that tale about Fortesquieu? You never heard it from him then, Travis?"

"I never knew him personally."

"You didn't?"

"No. The contract was drawn up and signed through an agent. I heard the studio was to let for the summer, liked it and rented it. The owner, I understood, had gone to America."

"So he had! I forgot! . . . Well, well! J. Fortesquieu was a queer fellow."

"Was?" said Travis.

"Didn't you know he went back on the freight list?"

"Good heavens, no!"

We all leaned forward.

"Well, he did," said DeJong, "and as I'm first officer I ought to know. I handled the bill of lading myself. . . . You rented in April?"

The Bachelor Dinner

"Yes, on the first.

"Then he died just before."

"That's queer," said Travis. "Not that it makes any difference to me, but I rather wonder——"

DeJong threw back his head and laughed. "That you hadn't been notified? Oh, he left an estate. There's some lawyer in charge. J. Fortesquieu had ways of his own. The last time I was in this studio—hm-m! . . . You've left things just about the same, I see, Travis."

Dan went on smoking and shrugged his shoulders. "Just about," he said, "down here at any rate. Up there I refitted." He gave a little wave of his hand toward the gallery.

"Oh, you did, did you?"

DeJong began to draw on his pipe with his head on one side, holding a lighted match to the bowl. As he puffed, he gave a swift glance around at the other men present. We were all silent, listening. The evening was still. From the garden outside came the scent of wistaria.

"By the way, Travis,"—DeJong raised his head suddenly and turned to our host—"Fortesquieu didn't happen to leave his wife here with you, did he?"

Dan gave a start and flushed.

"What do you mean?" he exclaimed angrily.

Fortesquieu's Wife

"What the devil do you mean by that, sir? . . . Fortesquieu's wife!"

At that moment the door at the end of the gallery above us moved slightly. It creaked on its hinges, and we all raised our eyes instinctively, simultaneously. Travis sprang to his feet.

"Excuse me," he cried, "just a second, gentlemen!"

With that he darted up the spiral staircase, and was on the gallery in a flash with his hand on the door-knob. It opened and then it shut again directly. Behind that door—the light was dim, so I could not be sure, but I thought I saw the face of a woman. I looked quickly at Barry. Had he seen too, had the other men? Or was it only imagination? DeJong said nothing.

Almost immediately the door reopened and Travis came back. He was pale, and his manner was moody, distraught. Without glancing at any of us, he came down the stairway slowly, and walking over to the long studio window, he began to lower the yellow curtains. He lowered them an inch or two in an absent minded way, staring out into the garden; then he pulled them up again— as far as I could tell, exactly where they had been before—and wound the cord over the hook. We watched his movements curiously in silence. The Count shrugged his shoulders.

The Bachelor Dinner

"Dites, Travees," he said, "is it that we dine without the cher docteur, or is it that we attend him?"

"We'll wait for him, I think," said Travis. He wheeled about suddenly and came forward, with an assumption of naturalness, almost of gayety in his manner. "That is if you do not object, gentlemen! Ménard is absorbed body and soul just at present. An experiment he has been working on for weeks, which is near its conclusion. He'll be down shortly. . . . You were saying, DeJong?"

Travis made a slight motion of his hand toward the first officer. His tone was courteous; but underneath, scarcely veiled, was a note as of menace. DeJong crossed one leg heavily over the other and puffed at his pipe. His head was tilted back against the cushion of his chair, and his eyes were fixed on the gallery above him. There was a look of surprise, almost of bewilderment, on his face.

"You don't mean to tell me!" he exclaimed. "Of all things! . . . By George, that is extraordinary! You've got a laboratory up there, Travis?"

"What's extraordinary about it?" said Travis. "Why shouldn't I have a laboratory?"

"You used the whole space, the—the— Did the agent know it? Jove! was nothing reserved, man?"

Travis stared at him. "Reserved!" he said.

34

Fortesquieu's Wife

"For Fortesquieu's w——" DeJong stopped suddenly as Travis held up a warning hand.

"That's all right, old man, that's all right! Don't get excited! Fortesquieu probably changed his mind. I only thought I'd tell you the story. Six months ago, the last time I was in this studio —well, it was a queer business, one of the oddest things that ever happened to me! And I'm not likely to forget it with that spiral staircase and door before me. A pretty bit of eighteenth-century carving, by the way, isn't it? Fortesquieu brought it himself from Italy. I knew him fairly well, poor fellow, fairly well; but still I must say I was astonished when— Sit down, won't you, Travis? For heaven's sake smoke, man! Take a cigar! You prowl around like a caged panther."

Dan gave a light, uneasy laugh and dropped back on the window bench. As he did so, I noticed that his glance for a fleeting moment followed DeJong's. The door above had opened a crack.

"Yes," said DeJong. "Toss over the matches, will you? Thanks! . . . When Fortesquieu's note was brought to the ship at Cherbourg, just after we'd anchored, I didn't know what under heaven to do. It read this way:

'DEAR DEJONG: Leave the ship at once if you have any regard for my honor. Come to me to-night. I am nearly distracted!

J. FORTESQUIEU,'

35

The Bachelor Dinner

His usually firm, rugged handwriting was all blurred over, and the J of his signature was lost in a splash of ink as big as a shilling. Now, what was I to do, gentlemen? As you know, for an officer to leave his ship is no laughing matter, and might easily lose a man his position. On the other hand, there was Fortesquieu, poor fellow, evidently in some dire dilemma! . . . Well, I took the note to the captain; and then, at his advice, wired to head-quarters. The answer came back, swift and laconic:

'Excused from service for forty-eight hours.'

Then I caught the boat express for Paris. It was raining heavily when the train arrived. A pitch-black night, not a star in the sky, and a drizzle of fog that hung like a great drop-curtain over the city, swallowing up the Tuileries, the river, the bridges, the island; only the towers of Notre-Dame, emerging grim and stark, ghostly, suggestive of the Morgue, crouched behind in its shadow."

DeJong stopped for a moment and looked about him, shaking the ashes from his pipe into the receiver. It had grown very dark by now in the studio. Only the dim outlines of the men's forms were visible, the cigar tips and pipe bowls gleaming like glow-worms.

"It may have been partly the fog," DeJong

Fortesquieu's Wife

continued, "or it may have been partly the tone of the letter—you may believe it or not, as you choose—but when I reached Fortesquieu's door, I stood before it like a shivering school-boy, afraid to ring the bell. What on earth could have happened? What awful thing must have happened before Fortesquieu, a sane, calm, level-headed business man, could have sent me off a summons like that? As I stood there, hesitating, the door was flung back and Fortesquieu himself rushed out on the landing.

'You?' he exclaimed. 'At last! I knew I heard the cab. Come in, DeJong, come in!... Thank heaven you were able to get your leave! It's eight o'clock now, and the others will all be here in a moment.'

'The others?'

'Yes, yes,' he exclaimed nervously, 'I'll explain! Sit down. Here's some rum and hot water! Take off your overcoat; it's drenched through. Help yourself!... Lord, the relief it is to see you!'

'What's up, old man?'

'Up!' he cried. 'Up!... Why, I'm engaged to be married!'

'The devil!' said I. 'You don't mean to have the assurance to tell me, Fortesquieu, that you've put me to all this trouble for the mere purpose of announcing a fool thing like that? What the deuce

37

The Bachelor Dinner

do you suppose I care, if you're engaged or married a dozen times over!'

At that he caught me by the arm, his fingers clutching mine like a vise. 'Sh-h, sh-h! Don't roar so! They may be out on the landing now! Listen, DeJong, you don't understand. It's the —the second time!'

'Bosh!'

'Don't get into such a rage! The circumstances are so strange, so extraordinary! I beg of you, have patience for only a moment. If you knew what I have suffered, the terrible things that have been rumored about me! Why, the whole American colony, they say, has been talking.'

'About you?'

'No, about—her!'

'Your fiancée, man?'

'No, no, DeJong; don't you understand? My— wife!'

'Fortesquieu! Well, I'll be— How in the dickens can you have a fiancée and a wife at the same moment? Are you mad?'

'That's just it,' he said earnestly, 'I shall go mad; I shall certainly go mad if this sort of thing keeps up much longer! That's just why I sent for you all, why I wanted you to be present when——'

He glanced nervously first at the clock, then up to the gallery.

Fortesquieu's Wife

'She's up there,' he said, making a little backward motion with his hand, 'It's been going on a long while now, DeJong. You never knew about it, did you? We'd been married eleven years, she and I. I fell in love with her when she was nothing but a slim slip of a girl, with her hair down her back in two long yellow braids. That was long ago in the Hackensack village days, before the money fever got hold of me. I was a wild enough fellow then, up to every prank that was going, set on leaving the farm and striking out for myself. How or what I didn't care; only the mad desire of the colt to get away, to slip the halter and be off on the gallop. The old man thought, and I don't blame him, that his youngest son was bound for the devil. So things went on from bad to worse. The situation soon grew intolerable. Every day, every week, every month, saw J. Fortesquieu slipping down hill a little faster.

And Madge—— All that time she'd been growing up steadily. Her braids were twisted high on her head now, like a golden wreath; and her eyes were blue as the corn-flowers in the meadows. At seventeen she was the belle of the whole village. Every man in the place was in love with her, from the bank clerk and the county attorney to the very louts and the farm-hands; and there was even a fellow from Pittsburg, they said, a rich young

The Bachelor Dinner

manufacturer, who had begun to follow her around like a shadow.

It's all up with me now, I said to myself, and the sooner I'm off the better. By Jove, I'll go West and strike out for myself! So I scribbled a note:

'DEAR MADGE: Meet me at the end of the lane to-night by the old elm, if you want to say good-by. I'm going away for good and all.

J.'

She won't be there, that's certain, I said.

At nightfall I went and stood under the elm; but I knew she wouldn't come. After a while I turned to go away, and just then I stumbled and looked up—and there she was! She was laughing at me.

'What's the matter, Jack?'

'Nothing,' I said, gritting my teeth. 'I hope you'll be happy with that Pittsburg fellow, Madge. Good-by.'

'You're really going?'

'Yes, there's been another row! I'm not cut out for a farmer, Madge. I can't stand it any longer. I'm going out West to be a miner, or a cow-boy, or something.'

'Are you?' she said. 'Are you, really? . . . Good-by.'

'Good-by—Madgie!'

'How much money have you, Jack?'

Fortesquieu's Wife

'Enough for the fare and a few dollars over.'

'Well, I've got enough for the fare and a few dollars over too. And if we starve, we'll starve together! . . . Come along!'

DeJong, she held her arms out to me then; and in that moment, something seemed to harden and tighten inside of me like a screw turned. From that second I was a changed man. She loved me, she believed in me, she clung to me—bless her! She gave up everything in the world, and followed a man who had been nothing but a curse and a failure; followed him nobly, followed him blindly.

For a year we worked together, we struggled together, and, just as she said, we starved together. Then the luck turned. The day it happened—I shall never forget it. We had left the mining camp behind us and were starting to ride on a lonely trail, intending to cross the mountain to a higher and smaller camp beyond, when we checked our horses to look at the sunrise.

'How yellow and radiant it is!' she exclaimed. 'How it shines—like gold! And the rays point there!' She turned as she spoke and flung her riding-whip over her shoulder. 'Dig where it falls, Jack, dig where it falls. The Sunrise Claim! We will stop here and stake it out and build our home.'

And we did, DeJong; we did just that. Almost at once we struck a belt of gold; as it turned out

The Bachelor Dinner

afterward, one of the richest mines in the country. In a short time we had machinery constructed—a large plant—and our fortune was made. For ten years we lived there in the midst of our miners, Madge and I, the happiest people in all the world. She was like a queen; the only woman in the whole camp and worshipped by all the miners, young and old. Then, one spring—when the rains came—she took a chill. It was all so sudden. In less than twenty-four hours she—she died, De-Jong. She died in my arms!

My God, man, I was nearly crazy! I remember nothing that happened for a long while afterward. They said I was down with a brain fever and raved like a madman. The weeks went by and the miners nursed me, turn and turn about, until finally, one day I opened my eyes, weak as a baby, and asked for Madge. They put me off. Then I asked again.

DeJong, you may believe it or not, as you choose —it sounds incredible, but when I asked the third time, they carried me to her. Six weeks had passed—six long weeks—yet they carried me to her.

There was the coffin, roughly cast out of metal, fashioned like a couch with a gold brick for a pillow. She lay on it with her eyes closed, her yellow braids about her, her cheeks slightly flushed, a red scarf flung across the white of her garment.

Fortesquieu's Wife

When I looked, I could have sworn she was actually breathing. But she seemed to be asleep. Then the miners told me.

The day that Madge died, an old woman had come to the camp. Everything was in wild confusion. The men were at their wits' end to know what to do, and I lay unconscious. So they called on the woman. She was a queer old hag, and seemed to be a squaw. Her mouth was toothless, her form was bent and crippled, her skin was wrinkled and brown like parchment, and her eyes were like black beads. She nodded when they explained the situation to her.

'Three days,' she said, 'three weeks, three months, three years? . . . Which?'

They could not understand what she meant, so they offered her money, anything, everything. Again she repeated the formula, muttering:

'Three days, three weeks, three months, three years? . . . Which?'

Still they could not understand and were puzzled.

'Do the best you can for our beautiful lady, the best you know how; and we will pay you well, whatever you ask!'

Poor fellows! They were beside themselves with grief, and through the wall came the sound of my raving.

The Bachelor Dinner

'Three years, then!' said the woman. 'Good! Bring me all the whiskey you have in the camp.'

'What?'

'Every drop of whiskey there is in the camp, and be off about it! Unless you are quick——'

They started and looked at one another. Whiskey!... DeJong, as you know, miners are invariably hard drinkers, and ours were no exception. The winter supply had only just arrived, dragged up to the top of the mountain at endless expense and trouble, on sledges. When that was gone no more was to be had. Every drop of the fluid was practically priceless.

'Either that,' said the woman, 'or——'

She shrugged her crippled shoulders. But before she could speak the men were gone; and they never hesitated. They rushed out wildly in all directions, calling in the supply—to and fro through the camp to the outermost corner—not so much as a single flask escaped. It was all brought in and laid at Madge's feet. No greater sacrifice could have been made, as all who know the life can bear witness. And they made it loyally, gladly, magnificently! The woman looked down at the still form on the couch; then she counted the whiskey flasks. Then she turned the miners out of the room and the door was locked. That was all they knew.

Fortesquieu's Wife

Twelve hours later they broke down the partition. Madge lay as I saw her, easily, naturally, with the flush on her cheeks. Strewn over the floor were the empty bottles. It was still as the grave and the woman was gone.'

Fortesquieu hid his face for a moment. Then he turned on me fiercely. 'That was two years and a half ago, DeJong! I left the camp and came over to Paris. She had always longed so to come to Paris. Well, I came, I brought her. The difficulties of transporting the coffin were endless, but with money to oil the wheels I managed; and here we have been ever since in the studio. We have never been parted!... You don't believe me?'

'No,' I said, 'Fortesquieu, frankly I don't. In the first place such a thing is impossible. In the second, the authorities would never permit it."

He sprang to his feet.

'You think me a madman, eh, DeJong? Tell me! You think me a madman? Don't go! Wait! I can prove it to you in a moment now—I can prove it to them. She is lying up there just as I told you.'

Again he made a backward motion of his hand toward the staircase.

'You see, man'—he spoke rapidly, feverishly—'if I had only been contented! At first for a while

The Bachelor Dinner

I was. She was there in the chapel. I didn't
open the coffin again, I couldn't; but I knew she
was there. Then later— You can't imagine how
lonely one gets, DeJong. Let me tell you—
there was an American lady. We used to be together. She was pleasant, sympathetic, and she
seemed to like me. I don't know, I am sure, how it
happened, but suddenly we were engaged. That
is how it was, that is why I sent for you in my
trouble, DeJong. I was nearly crazy! All of a
sudden everyone was talking. How the rumor
spread, heaven only knows, but they said there was
something strange about me; that I posed as a
widower, but my wife was still living, and I kept
her here, locked up in my studio! . . . Oh, the talk
and the fuss about it has been frightful. I tried
to explain, but not a soul would believe a word of
my story, not even——'

Fortesquieu rushed to the door suddenly.
'There, I hear wheels! They'll be up in a moment!
. . . DeJong, you'll stand by me?'

'I'll stand by you all right, Fortesquieu,' I said.
'Does the lady want to break the engagement?'

'She has broken it,' he exclaimed sharply.
'Didn't I tell you? She has broken it. She
wouldn't believe me. That is why I have invited you all here to-day! . . . Come in, please.'

The door opened slowly, and two ladies and a

46

gentleman appeared in the entrance. Fortesquieu looked at them, then he looked at me.

'That is why I have invited you all here today,' he repeated. 'Will you do me the favor of mounting this staircase?'

He went first and we followed in procession silently; the ladies ahead, the gentleman and I bringing up the rear. Fortesquieu crossed the gallery and opened the door."

DeJong stopped all of a sudden and looked at Travis.

"There was no laboratory there then," he said; "The place was fitted up as a mortuary chapel. Before the altar candles were burning, and beneath the candles stood a coffin on a dais. The air was heavy with incense. . . . Well, Fortesquieu faltered a moment; then he took a key from a ring in his pocket and hurried forward to the altar. We followed him closely. The light was dim and the scene was a strange one. Fortesquieu knelt on the dais, fitting the key into the lock of the coffin. His hand trembled, and his face in the candle-light had grown haggard.

'For two years and a half she has lain like this,' he said, 'and in all that time I only saw her the once. I have made other friends and followed other gods, and in the moment of trial they have all forsaken me. She would never have forsaken

me! She would never have doubted! Madge!—
Madge!' As he cried out sharply, he flung open
the coffin.

"What we saw there, gentlemen," said DeJong,
"what we saw there that night I shall never forget. She lay just exactly as Fortesquieu said—
the gold of her hair, the soft flush on her cheeks,
the red of the scarf flung loosely about her. Almost she breathed; she seemed about to waken.
It was extraordinary, it was marvellous! We all
stood dumb, like so many statues. Fortesquieu
crouched motionless, transfixed, on his knees; his
eyes riveted, his hands trembling, stretching out
toward her as if imploring forgiveness. The
emotion, the joy, the love in his face brought us
all of a sudden back to our senses. The lady
spoke first.

'Come,' she said in a whisper, 'we have no
place here—we have no right here! Let us leave
them together!' She turned softly and fled down
the staircase. The rest of us followed.

That was the last I ever saw of him." DeJong
hesitated a moment; then he knocked the ashes
out of his pipe and refilled it. "It was a strange
business, now wasn't it, gentlemen? And the
strangest part of the whole thing was that, three
years to the second from the time of his wife's
death, Fortesquieu died in this very studio, up

in the chapel. He was found one morning beside the coffin, crouched on the dais; and what he died of was never made certain."

DeJong looked up suddenly. "The authorities kept everything very quiet," he said. "There was some investigation, but what no one knows. He left some instructions behind, I heard. That is the reason"—he nodded carelessly toward Travis —"when I heard that you had refitted above, I was curious; but of course, what on earth would you want of the chapel? . . . By the way, Travis"—DeJong leaned forward—"You wouldn't let me go up there, would you? I must say, I should like to see what you've made of it."

Barry laid his hand suddenly on mine in the shadow.

"Did you see that?" he whispered. "Did you see that, McD? . . . What on earth is the matter?"

DeJong was on his feet, smiling strangely, undecided. Travis had leaped to the foot of the stairway. It was as if to intercept him. Just at that moment the clock began striking. Travis started; then he turned like a flash and touched a bell in the wood of the panel.

"Eight o'clock!" he said shortly. "I ask your pardon, gentlemen, for delaying the dinner. Ménard is detained; we will wait for him no longer. Let us sit down to table."

The Green Turquoise

AS the seven of us drew up our chairs to the
table there was a moment of rather awkward
silence. Barry Whittemore and I sat vis-à-vis to
one another; General Chatterton to the left of
our host, with Taglioni beside him; DeJong and
Count Nicot at the opposite round of the board.
The seat to the right of Travis was empty.

We unfolded our napkins. An elderly waiter,
with the precision and deftness of the trained
Frenchman, moved noiselessly about and poured
out the wines. As the lights went up, for the first
time, I saw the face of the General distinctly.

It was heavily, rather coarsely moulded, the
mouth hidden by a thick gray mustache, his eyes
small, very blue, and piercing—the eyes of a man
who was used to power, and from the look of his
chin he intended to have it. I glanced at Travis.

Although the types of the two men were utterly
different, in this one trait they were both alike—
they were natural leaders. Men of weaker stamp
would yield to their wills as inevitably as steel to
a magnet. What would happen in case those two
wills should clash? I caught myself wondering.

The Green Turquoise

The General, just then, was tucking his napkin into his waistcoat. Not a word had been spoken, when Barry suddenly leaned forward. He did it instinctively, he told me afterward, more to break the silence than anything else, and because the color happened to strike him.

"That's a curious ring you have there, General! I beg your pardon, but a turquoise like that is rather a rarity."

"Yes, er—really?" The General glanced carelessly over at Barry. "The workmanship is unusual. Quite so!"

"Indian, sir, if I'm not mistaken?"

"Exactly—Indian. As a matter of fact, Travis, do you know, I only got it the other day. The circumstances were rather peculiar."

"Peculiar?" said Travis.

He had an abstracted look on his face as he spoke, as of one whose thoughts have been miles away, called back with an effort. His tone was mechanical.

The General took a spoonful of soup before answering. "Excellent this, Travis—just the right flavor! It's wonderful what these French cooks can make out of just a medley of stuff flung together. You've got a new man?"

"No. That is—" Travis shrugged his shoulders. "I really don't know, General. Jean attends to everything for me! . . . Did you change the cook, Jean?"

His French, as he spoke it, I noticed was perfect, with a turn and an accent few foreigners have.

"Oui, monsieur."

The General threw back his head and laughed. "There's the difference, my friends, between the married man and the bachelor. You're a clever dog, Travis! You know when you are well off. If you had a wife now—ha-ha, my boy—you would soon have known if the cook had left!"

The wine-glass that Travis was holding shook slightly, and the red of the claret spilled over on the tablecloth. Barry gave him a quick look and again leaned forward.

"Excuse me, General—how very strange! Why, that stone in your ring is a green turquoise! It is a turquoise, isn't it? I am surely not mistaken. Did you ever see a green turquoise before?" He turned eagerly as he spoke, confronting the table. "Won't you hold up your hand to the light again, General? . . . There, look! It's a perfect beauty!"

"Are you a collector, sir?" said the General. "You know a good stone when you see one, do you?"

"Well—not exactly—no," said Barry. "But antiques, that sort of thing, they're a hobby of

The Green Turquoise

mine. You wouldn't let me—er— Oh, thank you!"

I stared at Barry in blank amazement. Antiques a hobby of his! Why, he couldn't tell an antique from a saucepan! His eyes met mine gravely, and he went on talking with the air of an expert.

"Now, a blue turquoise, General—of course we all know they are common enough; so are those just off color. They say any acid in the water will do it. But a green like this, it's extraordinary! . . . You have heard the legend about them, haven't you?"

"No, I can't say I have."

The General looked at my friend rather curiously. As Barry stopped, the other men glanced up from their plates, and the sudden interest aroused was evident.

"No? . . . Well, it's an odd superstition. Heaven knows how it originated! I heard of it first, years ago from an old French jeweller, a dealer in Marseilles. He said he believed it. If a turquoise, he said, is given in troth between two lovers, and one is faithless, the blue stone that the faithless one wears turns green. Just as this has, you see. The change is unmistakable, it occurs immediately; and through it each lover can test the other. Without words or scenes, simply at a

53

glance, they can tell how they stand beyond the shadow of a doubt. Very practical that—must save lots of trouble! It's an Indian legend."

Barry took up his fork carelessly. The roast had just been passed.

"Eh—an Indian legend? . . . What?"

"You never heard it before, General? Why, you surprise me! Among a certain hill tribe in India—I forget the name now—the turquoise is always used as a love-stone. The blue ones, those that have kept their color, are considered sacred; they are handed down from father to son and from mother to daughter. But the green ones, like certain scarabs in Egypt, they are cursed! They are blood-stones!"

"That's strange!" said the General. "You interest me, sir; you interest me exceedingly. Blood-stones—but why?"

"Because the one who is forsaken, whether the man or the woman, must take revenge. They're obliged to, you see. It's one of their social laws; no worse, after all, than some of our own! And when the stain is wiped out, the stone resumes its natural color."

"By George, is that true, sir? I've lived half my life in India, and I never heard that!"

"No? . . . You didn't?" said Barry.

"One of the hill tribes, you say? My word,

The Green Turquoise

then! Why, that would explain— This is most amazing!... Did you hear that, Travis?"

Barry stretched out his hand impulsively and laid it on the General's. "The name of that tribe! Wait a minute, wait a minute!...Jove, it's escaped me! Here's your ring, General."

The older man nodded and stared at Barry. He seemed to be excited.

"That's a strange coincidence, a most remarkable coincidence that you should have told me that, sir, just now! Why, it's years ago that the thing happened! Gwen and I were young officers, lieutenants together in the Indian service when he told me the story; and since then, 'pon my word, the entire matter had passed from my memory until just the other day, when I heard he was shot."

"Gwen?... Major Gwen?" exclaimed Barry.

"Yes, did you know him?"

"Oh, slightly—the barest acquaintance! Strange such a man should commit suicide. What possessed him to do it? It isn't often that a man of his calibre——"

"Suicide?" cried the General. "Gwen? Never. Where under heaven did you get that idea?"

"From the papers," said Barry; "the accounts all agreed. He was found in his summer-house where he worked in the mornings, his revolver beside him. He was unconscious then, but later he rallied, and when the surgeon arrived——"

"Yes—yes!" said the General.

"He confessed that he had done it in a moment of depression."

"The papers said that, did they?"

"Yes."

"Well, they lied."

"I'm sorry, sir; but the attorneys, Pennant and Co., Major Gwen's lawyers—I know them very well—and they told me the same. There was never any question."

"The attorneys lied." As the General said this his face flushed purple, and he brought his fist with a bang on the table. "I tell you, young man, I know what I'm saying—Major Gwen was no suicide."

Barry hesitated a moment. I nudged him with my foot under the table, and the General turned suddenly back to our host.

Travis was staring in front of him, twirling his salt-cellar; and Nicot was talking with DeJong in an undertone. Taglioni was eating.

"By the way, Travis— Eh, what's the matter? You don't look very fit!"

Travis pulled himself up with a start; but before he could answer, Barry broke in again persistently, irrepressibly. He was too good a lawyer to leave an argument high and dry like that with the proof in his hand. It was against nature.

"General Chatterton!"

"Well?"

"You're mistaken, sir. I'm sorry to have to tell you, but I was in London yesterday, in Pennant's office, and they showed me the paper signed by the Major."

"His own writing?"

"Yes, the few words in pencil where he makes his statement."

"That he shot himself? . . . What?" The General turned fiercely.

Barry nodded his head.

"Then, Mr. Whittemore, Gwen himself lied!" The voice with which the General roared this was evidently the one he used on the parade-ground. The very china rattled, and we all started back. "He did it to shield her! The papers don't know and the attorneys don't know; nobody knows. But the moment I heard the news I suspected, and now I'm sure to a dead certainty. He lied, I tell you, and he did it to shield her!"

"Who?" cried Barry.

"The woman, the woman who gave him the— Gentlemen, my friend is on his death-bed. He can never recover; he cannot speak himself, nor would he if he could. Any moment now the tele-

The Bachelor Dinner

gram may come. When I left him he was dying. To save his honor, to remove this terrible imputation that in his great-heartedness he has taken on himself, I will tell you the story. It is true as gospel so far as I know it—the inference is uncertain, but to me unmistakable. I will leave you to judge."

The General laid down his knife and fork, and we all did the same. Jean moved about noiselessly, changing the plates. Travis dropped the salt-cellar and looked up with interest. Barry settled comfortably back in his chair. He had the expression of the fisherman who, having once hooked his salmon, is willing to pay out all the line that it needs. His eye met mine and I thought he winked slightly.

"Yes, sir," said the General, "here you are, all men of the world, men of experience; and I'd take a high wager, you never heard anything like this before. The tale is so strange it's beyond belief. What I know I'll tell you—and then for the rest I'd like your opinion.

It began way back in the early seventies. Gwen and I were in the service together, and there wasn't a finer young officer in the army. He was a bit gay, just in the beginning, dividing his spare time between polo and dancing; but after the first year he was sent off to one of the remote hill stations,

The Green Turquoise

and for six months or more nobody saw him. When he came back he was utterly changed. Nobody thought much about it. The climate in India affects some temperaments. He did his work well and he kept to himself.

One night—it was the first queer thing I noticed —we were smoking together in my quarters. It was hot as hell, and he sat there shivering.

'Hey, Gwen! . . . Hello!'

'What's the matter?' he said.

'You must be in love!'

There had been some rumor floating about, that he was engaged to a girl in England who was on her way out. It was the wife of the colonel who started the rumor. It seemed she knew the aunt of the girl. 'Find out, Mr. Chatterton,' she said, 'can't you? He's as close as an oyster. Men are so inexplicable. Now the idea of you, his chum, not knowing!'

Well, I did it to please her. But when I tossed that remark over to Gwen, I did it off-hand, so that he could dodge it or not as he pleased. To my surprise, he sat there in his seat as if petrified. The look on his face was so strange that I was startled, and all of a sudden he gave a queer laugh, a laugh that chilled my bones.

'My word, old man, what's the matter?'

'Nothing,' he said, 'nothing! Look here, Chat-

The Bachelor Dinner

terton'—he spoke very low—'suppose you were engaged to a girl, a nice English girl, who had waited
for you for years and written to you faithfully;
and you knew, you couldn't help knowing, she
loved you! Suppose the date of the marriage was
settled—it was all arranged, and she was coming to
join you! What would you do?'

'You mean if——'

'Yes.'

'Great Scott!' I said.

'Do you think a fellow would be a cad?'

'Heavens, that depends! If he were sure of
himself, and it wasn't too late. I'd hate to do
it, Gwen, I swear, but if it were I, I'd break
the engagement. It's better, after all, for the
girl in the end. . . . Can't you let her down
gently?'

'But suppose'—Gwen's face went as white as
plaster—'suppose she'd started, sailed already;
she was coming out to join you!' He flung away
his cigarette and sprang to his feet. 'And suppose, Chatterton— God! suppose, if you can,
that you loved some one else!' He paced the room
fiercely. 'Some one you couldn't marry, you dared
not marry—you were too great a coward to dream
of marrying! Suppose yourself in the devil of a
fix like that! What would you do, Chatterton?
What, in all God's earth, would you do?' He came

over and clutched me by the shoulders, staring with a haggard gaze straight into my eyes.

'By Jove, I don't know, Gwen! That's a terrible business.'

'Think, Chatterton! I have racked my brains until my head is bursting! . . . Speak! Say something!'

'It isn't that fool of a Danby's wife, is it?'

'No, no!'

'Not the——'

'No, I tell you—nobody here! Nobody you know, or ever will know, or ever can know!'

His eyes met mine. For a moment there was dead silence between us.

It was then, all of a sudden, that I noticed his hand. He was wearing this ring, this same ring, gentlemen. I want you to mark it—and the turquoise was blue. It was blue then, believe it or not as you please. It was blue as the sea.

'The deuce!' I exclaimed. 'Where did you get that, Gwen? What a beautiful turquoise!'

You know how one changes the subject instinctively sometimes, in a moment of embarrassment? I did it to save him, to cover his emotion; but the very next moment I saw my mistake. He had grown still whiter, and had thrust both hands down deep in his pockets.

'Don't, Chatterton, don't!' he said. 'It's a raw

The Bachelor Dinner

wound still! You can't imagine what I'm going through, man. My dance is over now, and I've got to pay the piper. I'll do it, I'll do it, but I'd rather face hell!' He said it through his teeth. 'This is all I have left! Six months of happiness gone like a dream! This is all I have left!'

He stamped up and down the room for a long while, raving. I tried my best to quiet him, to bring him to his senses, but he flung me off and stamped on. It was a horrible night. The fellow seemed to have gone stark mad with his remorse and his memories. I never think of it now without a shudder. But at last he went off, about two in the morning; and the next day, when I met him on duty, he had himself in hand again. Except for his pallor and a certain curious blighted look, he seemed about as usual.

Well, about a week later the fiancée arrived. She was a tall, angular, ordinary enough looking English girl. There are thousands of them— blond-haired, red-cheeked, turned out of the same mould—good as gold and dull as ditch-water. Gwen took his hurdles nobly. They were married almost directly right there in the station, with the full pomp and ceremony of a military wedding. The colonel's wife arranged it.

'Poor dear young things!' she said. 'Not a relation between the two of them! Put on all

The Green Turquoise

your regimental frills and order the band. We don't have a marriage every day, and we'll give them a time that they'll always remember!' . . . They did too, but it wasn't the colonel's wife's fault." The General stopped suddenly and gave an odd laugh.

That wedding, gentlemen! The facts were all suppressed of course, and it never leaked out into the English papers at all; but the scandal there in India, in military circles—it was something appalling, and it all but cost Gwen his career. This is what happened.

At the door of the chapel, as Gwen led his bride out, suddenly a woman leaped from the crowd. It was all confused and over in a second, but I saw, we all saw, the dagger in her hand. Before any one could stop her, she had flung herself on Gwen. It was I who dragged her off. I've handled many a man in my life, and I've broken many a hard-mouthed horse, but, Jove—it took every ounce of muscle in me to grapple with that Indian girl! She was like a young panther—lithe, sinewy, panting with passion—as beautiful a creature as you ever laid eyes on!

She let out a torrent of jargon on me—stuff I couldn't make out except a word here and there. Gwen had reeled back. There was a patch of blood on his collar, and every one was screaming.

63

The Bachelor Dinner

Both he and his bride were surrounded directly, and then the thing was over. But one impression of that scene I shall never forget. The moment that he saw her, and the look on her face when she thought she had stabbed him—fury, love, triumph, passion, despair! As we dragged her away she hurled a sentence at him. I couldn't make it out then, but now I understand. She was pointing to his hand. Even as she struggled, fighting and raging like a trapped creature, she was pointing to his hand. *'Wah! Wah! Yama!** ... *Jo hoga, so hoga!'*†

That was a long while ago, gentlemen. Gwen was sent straight off to another part of India. The thing was hushed up; the Indian disappeared. It was years afterward before we met again, and then we'd both retired. He had a neat little place down in Surrey, and mine was adjoining. The friendship was resumed. Then, the other day— Mr. Whittemore has told you—Major Gwen was found shot."

The General took up his wine-glass and looked around the table.

"That's all very well," said Barry slowly. "It's an interesting story, but for myself I must say I don't follow your deductions."

"Nor I!" exclaimed Taglioni.

* God of Death.   † What shall be, shall be.

64

The Green Turquoise

We all shook our heads.

"How many years was it, General?" said Travis.

"Twenty or thereabouts. Wait a moment, if you please! The day before the shooting I was with him. We were in that same summer-house, when the gardener came out and brought him a letter.

'Another begging missive, I suppose,' Gwen said.

The writing was curious, and the postmark London. He opened it carelessly. All of a sudden I heard him give a cry. When I looked up, there he sat in his desk chair with his head in his hands, staring down at the paper. 'My God!' he said, and his voice was all gone, as if his breath had failed in his throat suddenly. As I sprang to my feet, the open sheet lay on the table before me and I couldn't help seeing. The writing was Hindustani. He covered it quickly.

'It's nothing, Chatterton,' he said. 'Don't be alarmed. I had a shock, just for a moment. It's nothing—a trifle! What were you saying?'

He looked very strange, I thought, but his face was hard to read. Whenever he chose, he could make it like a mask; and of course I asked no questions. We continued our discussion and then I went home. The next thing I heard he was shot and dying. They telephoned the news, and I rushed straight over."

"That was——"

The Bachelor Dinner

"Wednesday evening, Mr. Whittemore."

"You saw him?"

"Yes."

"You spoke with him?"

"I did."

"Then," cried Barry, "you mean the Major accused the——"

"No, no! He was dying, I tell you! They thought he couldn't live the night, but he was conscious—as conscious and in his senses, sir, as any man here. And this is what he said. His voice was so weak I had to bend over him, but I heard distinctly.

'Chatterton—you remember the turquoise? Take it! Keep it! And when she seeks you, tell her'—he gasped at every word—'it's all right, I understand. The stain is gone now! The stain is gone—now!'

Then he pointed to his finger.

I took the ring, obeying the look in his eyes and his motion; and almost immediately he relapsed into unconsciousness. It was coma, the surgeon said, and he would lie like that until the end. There was no hope of his reviving, so as important business called me to Paris, I took the night express and hurried away. I shall return as soon as the telegram summons me. That is all, gentlemen. Now, what is your opinion?"

The Green Turquoise

Barry crumbled his dinner roll reflectively.

"It's possible, of course," he said. "Stranger things have happened. But how do you figure that the woman got to England? And why should she wait twenty years for her revenge?"

The General passed his hand over his forehead. "Don't you see?" he cried. "You've hit the nail on the head exactly! The two things go together! She waited because she couldn't get there before. Now, this year for the first time——"

"The deuce!" exclaimed Barry. "I believe you're right! I forgot the Exposition. They brought an Indian village over and settled it there in the *White City*. That would be her chance, of course. Jove!... You made inquiries, did you?"

"At once."

"Well?"

"A woman from that Indian village had vanished."

We all started, and Barry leaned eagerly forward.

"The same day?"

"Yes. The body of an Indian was found in the Thames."

"An Indian woman?"

"An Indian woman."

Travis looked up quickly. I caught a glimpse of his face and turned away. He had shrunk

67

suddenly back as if struck. Barry gave an exclamation.

"Look, gentlemen, look—I swear!" He was staring at the turquoise. "It has changed color!"

We all gazed in astonishment. What he said was true.

At that moment the servant came in with a salver, which he carried to the General. "A telegram for Monsieur le Général."

"A telegram!" cried the General.

We looked at one another.

As the General's hand reached out for the message it trembled a little, and the light from the candles flashed on his ring.

The turquoise was blue. It was blue as the sea.

The Chess-Players

"THAT'S a very odd coincidence, General."
The murmur of excitement caused by the arrival of the telegram had about died away, and the business of dining had been resumed. The pheasant and salad were just being passed, when Nicot's voice broke the lull suddenly. It was a low voice, magnetic, with a carrying quality.

"All the same, coincidence or not," he exclaimed "for myself I believe it! To the rest of you the deduction may seem unlikely, but I've seen so many strange things in the course of my life! Where women are concerned everything is possible. Black skins or white, Asiatics or Europeans, it makes no difference. When their love, their passion, their jealousy is aroused, it is like the spark at the end of the gunpowder fuse! The strongest man if he takes fire—whiff, bang, gone, good-by!"

The Count laughed as he spoke.

"Take the Russian case of Klafsky for example —the most extraordinary affair that was. All the European papers were full of it a few years ago. You remember? In Paris the feeling ran very

The Bachelor Dinner

high, in Zurich and Geneva they held mass meetings, and in Milan there was a riot. But no one knew the real facts of the case; no one ever will know. The Russian police force were as mystified as the Central Revolutionists. Both were equally in the dark, and both equally swore vengeance. It was a curious situation."

"Klafsky!" cried DeJong, "Klafsky! Wait a moment, monsieur! . . . Where have I heard that name before? It sounds familiar."

"My dear sir," said the Count—he began to twirl the ends of his mustache impatiently—"of course you have heard it. Am I not telling you? At the time the thing happened, for a fortnight there, the press, the people, the whole world was interested."

"What!" exclaimed Barry. "You don't mean that Marx affair in Switzerland? The Russian police spy who——"

"The same," said Nicot. "No wonder you stutter. Who? What? Where? Why? Exactly. Was he Marx or was he Klafsky? Was he a police spy or was he a Revolutionist? . . . Those are the questions that two great counter organizations have been asking themselves many times over, and are still asking themselves to-day. So far as I know, they have found no answer, and they never will."

The Chess-Players

"I suppose there's a reason for that," said Barry.

The Count gave a quick glance over his shoulder. "Dites, Travees—are the walls thick?"

Travis nodded.

"No one beyond?"

"No one."

"Or upstairs there?" He pointed to the gallery.

The door was still ajar.

"That's all right," said Travis.

"Mais—" The Count made a protesting shrug with his shoulders.

"That's all right, Nicot."

"You are sure, Travees, no one will be lurking behind there to listen?"

"Certainly not." Travis flushed and his tone was short. His gray eyes followed the Count's for a moment. "Shall I send Jean away?"

He asked this with a gesture, under his breath.

"Eh bien, if you please—yes!"

We all waited in silence while Travis beckoned to the servant, whispering to him in French some order or other. Then the valet vanished, leaving the dishes.

"Thank you," said Nicot; "it is always wiser to take precautions." He glanced again at the gallery, but as Travis said nothing, he hesitated a moment and then went on. "You will give me your word of honor, gentlemen? I count on that. Not a breath, not a syllable of what I am going to tell you will ever be repeated, not even to your wives?"

DeJong interrupted him with a roar of laughter.

"Ha! ha! ha! You forget, don't you? we're all bachelors here, monsieur! You needn't worry about the ladies! Ha! ha! ha! I'm right, am I not, my friends—we're all bachelors?"

The laugh went gayly around the table, excepting for two. Travis was quiet; Barry had spilled the salt from his salt-cellar, and was engaged in scooping it up with the spoon.

"Good heavens, man!" he exclaimed irritably. "All this Russian secretiveness is enough to develop nerves in a cow! In America we shout everything on the housetops, and don't care a continental! . . . There are no police spies in Paris, are there?"

"Aren't there!" said Nicot. "My dear fellow, if ever you have occasion to speak of Russian affairs on this side the water, take my advice— whether it be Paris or Basle, Cologne, the Riviera, or Constantinople—look over your shoulder first and drop the tone of your voice low. Not for your own sake, you understand, but for those whose names you happen to mention. Many a tragedy

The Chess-Players

has come from careless talk in a train or a restaurant, a story told lightly, or an opinion repeated. Even with the utmost caution sometimes, a stray word let fall may prove a matter of life or death.

"You smile, sir?" he turned to DeJong gravely; "but unless you have personal acquaintance with these matters; unless the tragedies, their cause and effect, are brought home to you closely, specially, you cannot understand. For my part, my father was a Frenchman, my mother was a Pole, so I am three-quarter socialist and one quarter—" He looked from one face to the other slowly. "If the case had been reversed, I should have been three-quarter revolutionist probably instead. As it is, I sympathize and I comprehend. I do not approve. No!"

The Count's eyes flashed.

"I approve of no system, no society, no cause that puts a man in the position of Klafsky. Whatever his motives were, whatever his real character and purpose, it was a terrible problem he had to face. Whatever you may say of him, he faced it squarely. He did what he thought was right as he saw it. Can any man do more? There is no question of political sympathies in this case, gentlemen, because both sides abused and reviled him alike. He had lived between two fires for a dozen years or more—it takes a fairly

The Bachelor Dinner

brave man to do that—and the first time his foot slipped, they both let loose on him!

If Klafsky were alive now—pray heaven he is not—he is either lying at the bottom of some dungeon in Russia, or the Tribunal of Terror have him fast in their clutches. They vowed they'd get him sooner or later, that there wasn't a prison in all the Tsar's dominions strong enough or deep enough to hide him from their vengeance; so they may have succeeded. Either fate is unspeakable."

We all shivered, and again the Count glanced over his shoulder, swiftly, fleetingly up at the gallery.

"You give your word, gentlemen?"

As he said this, he stretched out his right hand solemnly, and we each shook it in turn, one after the other, across the table. Then the Count sat back and folded his arms.

"You probably think," he said, "most people do—that all Russian tragedies are enacted in Russia: but some of the most pitiful dramas I know have taken place right here in Paris; and in Switzerland, where the exiles congregate, the terrible stories I could tell you are countless. You remember when Bazilieff was extradited? He was tracked to Bern by a Russian spy, and then disappeared; lay low for a while like a fox under

The Chess-Players

cover. It wasn't until nearly a year later, the poor fellow tried to get marriage papers for the sake of his child that had just been born—to legalize the Nihilistic ceremony which had been interrupted. In a second he was pounced on. All those months some one had been watching, listening, waiting for just that very thing. They knew he would try it sooner or later.

I was in Bern at the time; and his young wife, the girl who had escaped with him from Warsaw, was at the station with the baby in her arms to see him taken back. Bazilieff, when his case was tried, only made one request. 'Extradite me, if you must,' he said, 'but marry us first.' The Russian Church refused. So the boy—who was just twenty-two they told me—was rushed back to Petersburg under strong police guard, and heaven only knows what became of him there! The girl and the baby remained behind. . . . The one little slip, you see; the mistake they made for love of one another. Their very honesty and morality killed them. Some one had talked.

The reason I mention this case to you, gentlemen, is because of Klafsky's connection with it. Nobody guessed it of course at the time, nobody imagines it now outside of official circles; but from this you can see the double nature of the man, and the blacker side of the life he was leading.

The Bachelor Dinner

Condemn him if you please. All Europe condemned him a few years ago, even the side he had been serving, even the side he was driven to serve—even Nadine. But before you judge, let me tell you what happened."

Nicot took up his glass of wine, emptied it, and set it down again on the table. The rest of us were listening intently. Again came that quick, instinctive glance around, searching the shadows; the Count then resumed.

"Yes—well, it happened one August. I had a friend with me, a man by the name of Reuss, from Bavaria, and we were travelling together through the Bernese Oberland; lounging in the valleys or climbing to the heights; doing a peak or two here or there, according to our fancies and the weather conditions. Reuss was a painter. You know his work perhaps, Mr. McD.?"

"Oh, very well," I said. "Of the Munich set I think, was he not?"

"Just so; a rank impressionist but a good fellow. He was making little magenta daubs of the Alps as we went along—regular blotches, with the paint stuck on all at sixes and sevens. His sense of beauty was a trifle distorted, to my mind at least; but for all that, it was he who first saw Nadine. This is how it occurred.

We were on our way to Interlaken; and the

The Chess-Players

steamboat from Thun was just out of the river, at the point where they turn, you know, into the lake. We had come on at Scherzligen with a big crowd, for those boats are always packed in the season, and were threading our way in and out through the benches, trying to find places. Suddenly I felt Reuss give a jog to my elbow.

'Sacrement! . . . Look over there, will you?'

'Where?' said I, staring about me. The confusion of tourists was anything but inviting.

'Straight ahead, at the bow! The chess-players —see! Push along, Nicot, I want to get a nearer view of her profile.'

'Bon Dieu!' I exclaimed.

We elbowed our way to the end of the boat.

Beyond the benches, at the extreme bow, was a little group of people, unmistakably Russians, three men and two women. Two were seated on the capstans close together, with their backs against the rail; the others clustered about them. The couple on the capstans held a chess-board between them, on which the eyes of all five were riveted. What struck me in a flash was the extraordinary absorption of the whole party. Evidently the tourists, with their crowding and chatter, did not exist for them. They were as unconscious of their surroundings as though alone by themselves on a desert island; the curious glances passed by

77

them unheeded. Either the panorama of snow mountains was an old story or they were indifferent to Alpine scenery, for not one of the group paid the slightest attention.

The afternoon was unusually beautiful; one of those clear, crisp days after a storm, and the horns of the Blümli glistened like silver. Off in the distance rose the Bernese range, Jungfrau, Mönch, and Eiger, all three silhouetted in white against the blue of the summer sky; the clouds drifting off from their summits like smoke, delicate, fleecy, hardly to be distinguished from the snow-fields themselves. There were white-caps on the lake; and the wind came whistling under the awnings, sharp, bracing, straight from the glaciers.

'Get nearer, can't you?' said Reuss softly. 'Push ahead to the rail. There's a woman ahead with a veil a yard broad; I can't see a thing! Sacré, but that's odd! Nicot, I say—it can't be a tournament.'

'They are Russian students, that's clear,' I whispered back; 'and they must be chess-fiends to play in the midst of a crowd like this. I'd give something to be able to watch their moves!... Let me pass please, madame.'

We edged still closer, beyond the last bench, and stood against the rail holding on to our hats. The Russians were now within close range. Reuss

The Chess-Players

began to gaze fixedly across at the Blümli, and I
followed suit, lifting my field-glasses.

'Colossal, isn't it?' he exclaimed with enthusiasm.

'Superb!'

'Couldn't have had a better day for the view!'

'No! . . . Ma foi, we're in luck!'

But all this finesse was lost on our neighbors;
they never turned an eyelash. From where we
stood now, we could make out the board. From
the look of it and the increasing absorption of the
circle, the game seemed to be a close one.

'Hist-st, Reuss,' I whispered; 'is that your
profile?'

'Yes,' he whispered back, 'the girl at the board.
That's a rare head! Look at the brow, and the
curve of the cheek and the chin. It's exquisite!
She's winning, too, if I'm not mistaken. I wish
I could get her on canvas like that, with the
hood of her cape drawn over her hair and her
curls blown in the wind! . . . How old would you
make her?'

'About twenty, not more. Sacrement, she is
winning!'

The girl suddenly lifted her eyes and looked
around. She held her opponent's black knight
in her hand, and her gaze sought that of the Russian who was nearest us. He was so near that as

79

their eyes met we got her expression, almost as if it were meant for ourselves. It was a curious one, and instinctively we wondered what the man was like, what his look could have been to have called forth the other. The girl's fingers trembled as she put the knight down; and she lifted her hand to her hood for a moment, as if to draw the folds closer. The other slowly advanced a rook; then she castled to the left and the game went on.

Her opponent was a slim, dark, anæmic young fellow, poorly dressed, roughly shaven, unhealthy looking. He also seemed nervous. Another man of the same type stood directly behind him. At his elbow, watching closely, was the other woman, heavily built, very Slavic in feature. She might have been his sister, and her gaze never wavered from the board for a moment. When the black knight vanished she gave a quick sigh—of relief or disappointment, it was hard to tell which.

The Russian who was standing beside the girl was a man of a different stamp, much older. He was a tall, athletic-looking fellow, with a loden cape slung over his shoulders, a cap on his head pulled down over his eyes, and something about him that was distinguished, apart, irresistible, compelling. One of those strong personalities that make themselves felt by their presence alone, without the necessity for speech or action. His

The Chess-Players

back was turned to us, so all we could see was his thick black hair slightly tinged with gray, and the freedom and picturesqueness of his poise as he stood there. He was smoking, and his face was bent toward the chess-players.

'What do you take him to be, Reuss—the tall one? He seems a sort of leader.'

'I don't know,' he whispered, 'but I've run across that fellow before somewhere. Where, for the life of me, I can't recall; perhaps it will come to me later! . . . Ha—Nicot!'

'Sh-h-h!'

'There's something up between him and the girl.'

'Looks like it.'

'There's something up between the whole lot of them, something more than we think.'

I nodded.

'There's more at stake than a mere game of chess. From the absorption of them all and the way they take it, you'd suppose it was a matter of life or death. Sacré! . . . That's queer!'

'What?'

'Pretend to be admiring the Blümli, Nicot; don't attract attention. Mon Dieu! . . . Did you see that?'

The young man had made a move with his queen; the girl brought hers forward. He advanced a

The Bachelor Dinner

black bishop; the girl moved her knight. Just as pretty a play as you ever saw. 'Check king!' she said.

At this exclamation, the tall man behind her threw away his cigar and made a motion as if to protest. His manner was strange, half-startled, like one who is fighting for self-control. The girl glanced up again. She was smiling faintly, and he laid his hand on her shoulder, coming nearer. When she felt his touch—it was plain to see—a little shiver seemed to run through her, and the blood rushed away from her cheeks and lips, leaving her pale almost as he was. Several more moves were made in silence.

With each play the intensity of the atmosphere seemed to increase. The waits were interminable, the manœuvres intricate, the outcome still uncertain. The two were well matched and were evidently playing a very strong game. But why such emotion? Why such extraordinary interest? It was out of all proportion.

Reuss shrugged his shoulders. 'These Russians must be an excitable set,' he muttered. 'Either that, or——'

'Or what?'

'They are playing for a purpose, and to win or lose means more than we think it does.'

Scarcely had he whispered these words in my

The Chess-Players

ear when the tall Russian turned and we caught
his face full. The agony expressed in it I shall
never forget. It was as if you saw a man in the
midst of a death struggle. Fear, even terror, were
written large in every feature, in every line, but
the fear and the terror were not for himself. The
struggle was not for his own life. Although we
were only a few feet away, and his gaze was straight
toward us, it was clear enough that he saw nothing,
he felt nothing, he heard nothing. His mind was
absorbed in something apart.

Whether the touch on her shoulder communi-
cated his thought to the girl or not, she began
shivering again; and all of a sudden she dashed
her queen forward.

'Check! . . . Check— king!'

The tone of her voice was indescribable. It was
triumphant like a battle-cry; and then in the
midst her breath seemed to fail her. Her opponent gave a quick exclamation, which the man and
the woman behind him echoed. It seemed one
almost of satisfaction.

Instantly, as if stunned, the tall Russian passed
his hand over his eyes, hiding them from the light.
It was the gesture of one who is drawing on a
mask. Then his hand dropped, in a flash he was
changed. The expression was gone and his manner careless.

The Bachelor Dinner

'She's winning,' said Reuss; 'and for some reason that tall fellow there, the leader— Parbleu, now where have I seen him before? . . . Look, Nicot!'

The girl had thrown back her head with a laugh, an odd little laugh, like a child half-pleased with itself, half-frightened.

'*Boje moi!*'* she cried, 'it's check-mate!'

For a moment all five of them seemed transfixed. Nobody moved, nobody spoke; they all stood staring down at the chess-board.

'That's a funny thing,' said Reuss softly. 'She's won sure enough, and she's pale as death! I don't understand this exalté strain. Why don't they congratulate her? What's the matter with them?'

Before I could answer, the spell broke.

The Russians began to talk excitedly together, gesticulating freely. One of the young men folded the chess-board up, slipping the chess-men into his pocket. The boat had just left Beatenbucht. As we watched, the girl rose slowly, unsteadily to her feet, and drew aside a little, back toward the rail where the tall man was leaning. The two put their heads close and they spoke in a whisper, but Reuss and I were very near. We understood Russian and we could not help hearing. This is what they said, word for word, as I remember it; the girl's voice first, soft as a breath:

* My God.

84

The Chess-Players

'Well—it's settled now, Marx.'

The man muttered something.

'Don't worry. It shall all be carried out just as you planned, to the very letter. Can I not do it as well as he? Why are you sad?'

'You are too young, Nadine, for this sort of business. You ought not to have drawn for the game at all. If I had dreamed— But Mieke is one of our best players, and he told me, he swore to me——'

'I know,' the girl interrupted contemptuously; 'he wanted to do it himself. It was she!' A little backward thrust of her elbow indicated the other woman, who was still talking, gesticulating behind them. 'She was frightened for him. The fool! Bah—they're poor stuff for patriots! I'm not afraid, Marx. I'm not that sort.'

The man gave her a sudden strange look, half proud, half tender, inscrutable; and his fist clenched as it rested on the rail.

'No,' he said, 'you're not—you're not, Nadine. You've got more courage in that little finger of yours than ten of Mieke put together. And you'll need it all to-night, all the nerve you have, child! ... Are you sure of yourself?'

'Yes.'

'You won't flinch?'

She threw back her head and her eyes flashed up

85

at him. He studied them for a moment, staring down into their depths.

'Regardless of consequences—remember.'

'I remember.'

The girl laughed out, but her lip we saw was quivering. The man made a sudden movement as if to put his arm around her, a movement checked half-way as he realized the crowd. That the two understood one another was evident. The absolute trust in her face was beautiful.

'We're nearly there,' he said; 'we'll be in Interlaken directly. You know where to meet me to-night—and when?'

'The pavilion—eight o'clock—on the Harder path. You will bring the——'

'Sh-h!' he whispered, looking over his shoulder. 'Yes, I'll have it all ready. You're to go to the Kursaal, you know, straight from there.'

'Mélikoff is certain, is he?'

'Chut!... He has ordered a table reserved, and you're to have the next, number 24.'

As the Russian said this the girl blanched, shrinking back with instinctive recoil as from a blow. And then to our amazement we saw that she was trembling. There could be no doubt of the fact this time. In every limb, in every muscle, she was trembling like a leaf.

Whether the man noticed or not, we could not

tell. If he did, he made no comment. There was silence between them. The two stood side by side against the rail, staring down into the water.

By this time the boat was approaching the pier and the passengers began to move toward the gangway. Reuss and I went off to attend to our traps. It was all confusion. When we landed finally, hurrying along to escape the line of porters, we scanned the throngs in vain. The Russians had vanished."

Nicot stopped for a moment, filled up his glass with wine, and took some lettuce on his fork. He glanced around the table.

"This tale doesn't bore you I hope, gentlemen?"

Travis leaned forward, pushing the paprika toward the Count's plate. He looked preoccupied, I thought, but his tone was full of warmth.

"Go on, Nicot, go on! . . . But eat, man, first; there's no hurry."

"No, no!" said Nicot. "The servant may be back."

"That's so!" exclaimed Barry. "We're all on pins and needles, Count! By George, I remember distinctly when the picture of Marx first came out in the papers. Cossack type, wasn't he? Strong-featured, dark-browed, striking-looking fellow; and Nadine a pretty little wistful-eyed thing? Not much of the criminal about either one of them.

The Bachelor Dinner

He didn't look a traitor, and as for that child—well, you can't tell much from a newspaper print."

The Count shook his head.

"Nor from the human countenance either, study it as you may. I dare say you will bear me out in this, Mr. Whittemore. Far from understanding others, we shall probably be puzzled by ourselves some day. As far as I can make it, in any very strongly developed individuality there are a number of different characters involved. Which of them finally wins out is determined by what—influence, circumstances, training—who can say? With Marx they had all combined to make him what he was, up to a certain period. He didn't choose his career. Nature gave him certain talents; his country recognized and used them. To earn his bread he started—was forced, you might say—along a certain road, just as most of us are. The line of least resistance or the line of most, according to our cravings. With him it was the latter case. Struggle, danger, excitement —they were the very breath of life to him. His nerves were strong, his wits were keen, and he tried to serve his country; did it, too, for twelve years, there's no doubt about that! Spy, agent as he was, he did his country good service. And then came the cross-roads; then came Nadine.

That I should have happened to be present in

The Chess-Players

his life at that critical moment was curious enough. Still more curious, perhaps, that I witnessed the struggle. And the way it happened, gentlemen, that was the most curious part of all—the reason why, personally, no matter what the world says, I could never judge him harshly. Hearing, seeing what I did that awful night in Interlaken, watching a man's soul bared as it were, writhing, agonizing, on the rack, in torture—who am I to fling a stone? Who are you? Who are any of us? We can only be thankful to have escaped the test ourselves.

Well, that evening Reuss and I, of course, were ignorant of all this. We proceeded to our hotel, a small one, not far from the East station, and dined quietly under the plantain trees, looking over toward the Jungfrau. We were too tired and hungry to talk much, and it wasn't until the coffee that Reuss suddenly gave an exclamation and clapped me on the shoulder.

'Sacrement, Nicot!'

'What?'

'I know now where I've seen him.'

'Who?'

'The Russian—that tall fellow.'

'Mon Dieu! . . . Where?'

Reuss gave me a queer look. 'You heard that conversation—yes? Odd, wasn't it? Did you understand the trend?'

The Bachelor Dinner

'Not particularly. They seemed to be mixed up in something, and the chess figured as a blind. What did you make out of it, Reuss?'

'Why they're Nihilists,' he said; 'they belong to that Central Revolutionary set. Those two were drawing lots there on the boat over the chess-board, and the little girl won. She'll be up to some deviltry to-night. I shouldn't be at all surprised if she meant to kill Mélikoff. He's here in Interlaken. I looked it up in the *Fremden-blatt* before I came down. A regular old Tartar too, with a list of crimes at his door. The only wonder is that they've let him live so long. There's her chance! The Kursaal, the table next reserved! Parbleu, Nicot, what shall we do? We'll have to put a spoke in their wheel somehow.'

'Call in the police,' I said.

'Not enough to go on, man.'

'Then—' All of a sudden a thought struck me. 'Here, I have it! You go to the Kursaal, Reuss, and I'll try the pavilion. If you keep an eye on table 24, I'll do the same with that couple up yonder. Eight o'clock was it—the Harder promenade?'

'Yes. There's time enough still.'

'All right. When that interview takes place I'll be present. I know that pavilion. We'll find out, Reuss, between us, and save the old Tartar

90

from his fate a while longer. Fancy that sort of thing in peaceful little Interlaken!'

Reuss drew his brows together.

'It isn't the plot that puzzles me,' he said. 'I've run up against these people before and I recognize their ways. The girl's a tool of course; an excitable child, full of visions and fancies. You could see for yourself she was wax in his hands. Why, she'd walk into hell at a glance from that man! No, it's the chief himself that disturbs me—their leader! What was it the girl called him, Nicot?'

'She called him Marx.'

'Exactly—Marx! Well,' Reuss gave a strange laugh, 'the last time I saw him—I remember it now perfectly. It was six months or so ago, and I was painting the portrait of Glazov, ex-Governor of Elisabetpol, and a man of high position. He had something to do with the secret police, just what I don't know; but one day—it was in his private salon in the hotel at Nauheim —he was sitting to me. Sacré, how it all comes back! Suddenly there came a light tap at the door.

'Come in!' said Glazov. 'Is that you, Klafsky?'

And in walked this fellow with a portfolio under his arm. The very same man, that I'd swear to. The same build, the same swing to his shoulders,

The Bachelor Dinner

the same deep-set, piercing eyes, the same strong, vibrating personality.

Glazov excused himself for a moment, and the two proceeded to go over the portfolio right there before me. You know, Nicot, it's my business to study faces. Once I've studied them I never forget. That Klafsky was an agent, a Russian police spy reporting to his chief. They went over a long list of names together; and after some they put a cross, and after some they put a question. Whatever the report was, Glazov looked pleased as Punch.

'You'll get an order for this some day, Klafsky; you're the best man we have. Why during the last years, since you've been on the force, every one of their schemes has miscarried. Thanks to you we've foiled them all, one after the other. If it hadn't been for you—the Minister of Education, the Minister of the Interior, the Vice-Governor of Ufa, Prince Androkof, the Chief of Police of Vladikavkaz, the Grand-Duke Boris himself, and hosts of others—they were all doomed men, and they owe their lives to you.'

With that Klafsky made a low bow and went out. But that expression on the General's face, you can see it in his portrait now—the look that Klafsky brought there, the look of the cat when the bird is in its claws. It was Klafsky put the

The Chess-Players

bird there. And now—ha-ha! His name is Marx, is it? A revolutionist! A leader! . . . Do you follow all this, Nicot?'

'No,' said I, 'I don't. It's a damned queer business. But if he's luring that Russian girl on to her death! These provocative agents, I've heard of them before—they are perfect devils! Good-by, Reuss, I'm off. That Harder path will be a dark meeting place to-night. Don't forget the Kursaal!'

'Bah, Nicot! It's not Mélikoff I'm worried about —it's the girl! If that fellow really is Klafsky, why he'll head her off himself. The moment she's in deep enough, caught in his trap, he'll hand the proofs over secretly to the Russian police. She'll be in prison for life, just as quick as that—and she'll never know what struck her! Mélikoff! Parbleu, he's safe enough. They'll never let her touch him! . . . Well, good-by, Nicot! Good luck!'

"Gentlemen," the Count paused; "when Reuss and I parted that night—he sipping his coffee on the hotel terrace, waiting for the Kursaal; I striding down the Höheweg off into the darkness —we both little dreamed what we had before us. The moon, which had come up earlier in the evening, had gone under a cloud, so once out of the village it was black as pitch. The trees along the path loomed up like gaunt spectres. The forest

The Bachelor Dinner

stretched ahead mysterious and vast, silent as the grave. Below were the lights in the valley twinkling, above were the stars, beyond were the snow peaks. So I groped my way upward. The walk is twenty minutes, but it seemed hours.

You know that pavilion, don't you? It stands on a ledge overlooking the valley, and is charming in the sunshine; but at that time of night, you can imagine, the place was lonely as a cave. I stole in on tiptoe and hid myself in a shadowy corner, and waited and listened. It was nervous work. The waiting was even worse than the walk. It was too dark to see my watch-face, and I dared not strike a match. Was it eight o'clock—was it past? Were they coming? Was it the wrong pavilion perhaps? There was another beyond. Had I misunderstood, or had something kept them?

Just as I was asking myself these questions, standing first on one foot then on the other, peering out into the open space at the head of the path, all of a sudden a shadow crossed it. It passed so quickly I could not be sure—and then came another. The shadows flitted across the entrance of the pavilion. A large one, a small one. And then, I could see nothing, but I heard breathing. The smaller shadow seemed to be panting.

'Sh-h-h!'

The Chess-Players

The hiss was so close that I started back.

'Did you hear anything, Marx?'

'Chut!'

'It must have been the leaves crackling.'

'No! It was a movement.'

'Perhaps it was mine.'

'Perhaps!... Come nearer, Nadine, come nearer! Tell me, you would go anywhere, you would do anything that I told you—would you?'

'Yes, Marx.'

'No matter what the risk, no matter what the consequences—life imprisonment, even death?'

'Yes, Marx.'

'You would brave all this at a word from me?'

'Yes—Marx.'

'Why would you, Nadine?'

'For the cause's sake,' said the girl faintly. I could tell from the tone that her breath was still fluttering, but the words were unmistakable. 'Are you not our chief? You have suffered everything, you have braved everything. You are our leader; and there is no one in all the revolutionary party who has done what you have done, who has been what you have been. Have you not planned the attacks for years now? And have we not always followed your call, blindly, unfalteringly—at a demi-mot?'

'You have, Nadine! God help me, you have!'

The Bachelor Dinner

The man's voice came suddenly hoarse, full of passion.

'You trust me so much then? . . . Ha!' he laughed aloud roughly. 'You trust me as much as that, do you? Speak! . . . Why don't you speak?'

'Yes, yes—I trust you.'

'Come then, *douscha moja*,* sit down beside me. Put your hand in mine and let us look at the stars together. The night is too beautiful for the Kursaal, for vengeance! Forget it, little one. I love you. I love you as I never loved a woman before. Come nearer. Put your head on my shoulder. I love you!'

The girl gave a low cry. Whether she resisted him in the darkness I could not tell. The man went on talking, pleading, in rough, passionate Russian phrases. 'If you trust me as much as that, *douschka*,† then you love me too! You are so dear to me, so dear to me. God! Come closer! Let me look at your face, let me read your eyes, let me kiss you on your lips!'

For a moment or two there was silence in the pavilion, and all I could hear was their hurried breathing. Then the girl seemed to rouse.

'Is it time to go? Hark! The music has just begun in the Kursaal. Don't you hear it from here? . . . Let me go, Marx, don't hold me. You

* My little soul.   † Soul.

are trying to test me, dearest. You think I'm afraid?'

'Stay with me,' said the man.

'Let me go—Marx.'

'Is the murder of Mélikoff more than my love?'

'Murder!' The girl started so that I felt it from where I stood. 'Murder! Why, hasn't the Tribunal tried him fairly and condemned him? Wasn't it you who planned it all, who signed the paper? Didn't you give out the orders yourself? What do you mean?'

'Nothing,' said the man. 'I've changed my mind, that's all. The orders are revoked.'

'But the vow, Marx—you forget I am bound!'

'No matter.'

'It is too late now! You have telegraphed my name to head-quarters as the winner of the tournament. The committee will expect another wire to-night. To back out at the last moment like this—you know what that means, Marx? You remember what happened to Tatiana?'

'I do,' said the man. 'God help me! God help me!'

Just as he said this, the moon broke from behind the clouds; the rays fell across the path, illuminating it as with a search-light. At the door of the pavilion stood the two close together. The man with his arms stretched out to the girl, his face

The Bachelor Dinner

white and haggard, full of despair—and she gazing up at him like a startled bird. A strange scene, gentlemen!"

The Count hesitated.

"Up to that time, the affair had turned out very much as I had supposed. Whether Klafsky loved the girl or not, he was holding her back, just as Reuss said he would. Mélikoff's life was as safe as yours or mine; so at least I thought then. But what were the fellow's intentions toward Nadine? That he meant to hand her over—I never doubted it a moment. And then, my friends, the unexpected happened. Klafsky broke down.

Whether it was the look of adoration and loyalty in the girl's eyes, or whether it was his conscience awakened at last, heaven only knows! Suddenly he buried his head in his hands. It was the most intimate, the most searching, the most terrible confession. He told her everything, he bared his life to her, he never spared himself for a single second; and the girl stood there stock-still and gasping. It was as if he were thrusting a knife into her heart.

Those two figures in the moonlight I shall never forget. The shadowy path, the black outline of the mountains beyond, the pallor of their faces standing out against the darkness—and that voice, tense, low, broken, like a cry through the night.

The Chess-Players

The tragedy of the situation, the hopelessness seemed to catch him by the throat. From the first syllable to the last the girl scarcely breathed; but her face spoke for her. He looked into it, read and accepted the verdict. For a moment or two the silence was ghastly.

Gentlemen," said Nicot, "what you would have done in my place I don't know; but crouching there hidden, watching those two, listening to what was never meant for any ears but hers, I felt like a thief. For any third person to be present unknown at such a scene as that, it seemed abominable, like desecration. You may blame me, perhaps, in the light of what followed. I turned my back on them and stole away without a sound.

What happened afterward up there in the night no one knows, no one ever will know. Whether she forgave him, whether she won him over, whether he paid it as the price of her love, or whether he tried to prevent her and couldn't. I have puzzled over that question for years, and am no nearer the solution. One hour exactly after I reached the hotel, Reuss came rushing in pale as a ghost, with his eyes almost starting out of his head.

'Great heaven, Nicot! Have you heard what's happened?'

The Bachelor Dinner

'Mon Dieu! . . . What?'

'Mélikoff has just been shot!'

'Shot?'

'At the Kursaal, right in the midst of the music! Every one was very gay, drinking their beer and listening to the jodlers. I had been watching the General all the evening. He was with a large party, very near me; and the table behind, number 24 was empty, the only unoccupied table in the place. All of a sudden came the crack of a revolver, from somewhere right out of space it seemed—so sharp, so sudden, so near! Everybody sprang to his feet in horror! And there lay Mélikoff with his arms across the table!'

"Well—" For a moment or two the Count was silent. "That was Reuss' report, word for word, and the rest of the story you know, gentlemen. It was all in the papers. Nadine was arrested, Klafsky disappeared. Mélikoff, poor fellow! He deserved it, but then——"

"Dead?" exclaimed DeJong.

"No, no!" said the Count impatiently. "Didn't you read the account, my friend? No more dead than you are. As a matter of fact it was fright that knocked him over. The General will tell you, in battle sometimes it happens that way. Mélikoff, the old sinner—his life had been threatened a score of times; and when he heard the crack, of course he thought he was gone, and fainted away out of sheer terror. That ball—" the Count laughed, "why didn't it kill him? . . . My friends, that ball was a blank cartridge."

"What? . . . No! . . . You don't say!"

The exclamations went around the circle.

"Exactly. That part of it wasn't mentioned in print. The fact never got out, but it's true for all that. The whole affair was hushed up by the authorities there in Interlaken. Nadine was whisked away. And then, forty-eight hours later, all Europe was ringing with the news. You remember? The news, the secret, gentlemen, that only her ears and mine had heard—Klafsky's confession.

You read all about it, didn't you? The Russian government was furious. They had lost one of their best agents. Their trump card was taken, their hand forced, their trick exposed. Naturally they vowed vengeance. As for the Revolutionists, they were roused to a man! The entire party, especially those who had followed Klafsky's leading, when they realized—imagine! Twelve years they'd been his dupe, they'd been playing his chess-games! Imagine what they must have felt! Heavy tragedians in spirit, and all their dramas, thanks to Klafsky, one after the other, turned into a farce! They were mad, they were crazy. If they could have gotten their fingers on him— sacrement, they'd have torn him to pieces!"

We all instinctively gave a shudder, and the Count glanced behind him.

"Yes, between you and me! We don't know of course, but with Nadine in prison— I may be wrong!"

"You mean," said Barry thoughtfully, "if Klafsky were alive, he wouldn't have deserted her?"

"Just that," said the Count; "And yet the extraordinary part of it is, the part that bothers me the most—I can't believe it of her, and I won't; and still it's the only thing to believe. Who was it told the secret? It wasn't Klafsky, it wasn't I, so it must have been——"

"No," said Barry, "not necessarily."

"How then, my dear sir?" The Count leaned forward and his face was flushed. "You don't suppose for a moment that Klafsky himself——"

"No, no, I don't."

"Or that I— Parbleu, man!"

"Of course not!" Barry laughed. "Not you, Count, not you. But that night you and Reuss talked it over, I dare say?"

"We did, yes!" said Nicot.

"If you will think for a moment, monsieur. The news came out in the German papers first;

you must recall that. I wondered at the time
why an incident in Switzerland——"

The Count gave a gasp.

"Reuss?" he cried, "Reuss? I never dreamed
of such a thing."

"Most likely thing in the world," said Barry.
"From the mere fact that the girl carried out her
programme, I knew directly that *she* had never
spoken. And what you say about the blank cartridge—Jove! That's a very pretty point! Klafsky must have hit on that loophole in desperation
as a final resort, and yet it didn't save her. What
a tragic story! She in prison, and he—dead, you
think, Nicot?"

"Dead, or worse!"

There was silence for a moment around the
table, and then DeJong lifted his glass suddenly.

"Gentlemen," he said, "in August, three years
ago, two Russians were found hidden in the hold
of a merchant ship. They were stowaways, a man
and a woman; and how they got there has always
been a mystery. I was captain at the time, and
the ship was on its way to America. They were
brought before me and they told me their story.
The choice was mine to make. They were utterly
at my mercy, and they both knew it.

Two roads stretched before them. The one
led to Siberia, a life of torture, a death of misery.

The Bachelor Dinner

The other to America, freedom—with the chance to start afresh.

Here's to the Chess-Players! . . . A better life beyond the sea!"

The Fourth Generation

SCARCELY had the last clink of the glasses ceased when all at once the Count sprang to his feet. "There," he said, "I knew it, I felt it! There's a woman behind that door, Travis!"

He stood looking up at the spiral staircase, pointing to the gallery with his finger. "Hush! . . . Diable, man, what did I tell you!"

It was true. We all listened; and distinctly, from above somewhere, there came a rustle, the swish of a skirt.

"Who is it?" cried Nicot. He was white as the table-cloth.

The rustling stopped. We could not be sure, but footsteps seemed to be lightly retreating. An exclamation went around the table. Simultaneously, instinctively, we all leaped up, grasping our napkins, peering into the shadows. A strong draught was blowing, whether from the window or above we could not tell; but all of a sudden—it was like a black pall thrown over our heads—the candles went out.

Now whether it was the strain of the Count's story, or that instinctive revulsion as from med-

ieval horrors that the Russian spy-system ex-
cites in a foreigner, I don't know, but for a second
the entire group stood as if paralyzed. Travis
spoke first. His tone was cool, unnaturally so.

"Got a match, anybody?"

We all began fumbling.

One after the other, a scratch, a fizz, first one
side, then across the table; finally Barry managed
to get one lighted.

"Shut the window, some of you fellows," he
exclaimed, "or the door! Quick!... By Jove,
what a gale!"

He was holding the match to the candle-wick
nearest him, protecting it with his hands. In the
flickering light everything looked large, unnatural,
ghostly. The seven figures flung seven shadows;
they stood out black, grotesque against the walls.
The shadows and the figures were all mixed together, moving like phantoms.

"Hurry up," cried Barry, "I can't hold this
match here forever! What the devil is the——"

He stopped suddenly with his head turned and
his mouth wide open. Our eyes instinctively followed his gaze. The draught had ceased.

On the gallery with his arms folded on the rail,
leaning over, a cigarette between his teeth, and
the most nonchalant, amused, quizzical look that I
ever saw on a human countenance stood——

The Fourth Generation

"Mon Dieu!" cried the Count. "Why I could have sworn— Sacrement! Was that you, Jacques Ménard?"

"Well, who did you suppose it was?" said Travis. He seemed relieved, a little excited. "Come down, Doctor. All through, are you? How is it going? You must have the whole place open up there. Anything wrong?"

The new-comer laughed and came down the staircase.

"I thought I smelt roast pheasant," he said. "Hand over a slice, Travis, and a glass of— claret, is it, or port? Yes, that will do. I just came to stretch my legs a bit and get a bite to eat, while things come to a head. Sorry to have startled you all, gentlemen. My word, but you looked like a lot of darkies who'd been robbing a chicken-roost, caught in the act! What have you been up to, eh? That's enough, Travis, much obliged!... Telling stories—ghost stories?"

The manner of the man was so easy, so genial, he was evidently so entirely at home on the ground, that nobody thought of any further introduction. There was something about him whole-souled, magnetic, an atmosphere. In a moment one seemed to have known him for years. As he began on the plateful with which Travis supplied him, he ate rapidly, heartily, like a hungry boy.

The Bachelor Dinner

Whatever convention may still have existed in the room when he entered, whatever formality, such as might be supposed to die hard among strangers, they were gone in a flash. The feeling of good-fellowship, cheer, was instantaneous; and he was the centre. As he ate we all watched him.

He was wiry of frame, rather lean than large, every bone, every muscle alive with energy; the very blood in his veins brimming over with life, vitality, purpose, a reason for being. His face, when you took it feature by feature, was ugly, there was no doubt about it; but so frankly, so strongly, so originally ugly that it charmed you. The eyes small, of uncertain color, the massive brow with its juts and ridges, were the eyes and the brow of the thinker, the delver into secret wisdoms and mysteries of which the mass of mankind knows nothing. A great man, every one of us felt that instinctively. The only person unaware of the fact was himself. He began on that pheasant with voracity as if he had not seen food for a month, and proceeded to satisfy himself without a word or a glance around him, as unconscious of arousing personal interest as if the rest of us had been so much furniture. In this very unconsciousness lay his fascination.

"No, no," he made a gesture toward Travis; "don't ring! This bird does very well for me.

The Fourth Generation

A little more claret if you please! Thank you.
My word, I was hungry!"

"No wonder," said Travis. "I should think you
would be. You were up with the sun this morning, and you haven't been out of the laboratory
since! . . . Any luck?"

"We'll see, we'll see!"

The Doctor was evidently too absorbed for
further answer, but in an incredibly short space of
time the pheasant was finished off; there was nothing left to show but the bones. He emptied his
glass of wine and came back to earth again.

"So," he said. "Now give me a cigar, my
friend; I'm going to enjoy myself until I'm dis-
lodged. Go ahead with your ghost stories."

He looked over at Nicot and laughed as he
spoke.

"Thought I was a spook, eh? Wish they were
all as solid! The psychical people wouldn't have
any show. What were you giving them?"

"Oh, nothing much, Doctor; just that little tale
about Klafsky. What do you think?" Nicot
drew nearer and lowered his voice, "Mr. DeJong
has been saying that he and the girl escaped
to America; they've been there all this time together. Curious business! We were just drinking to their health and moral regeneration when
you walked in. As a matter of fact——"

The Bachelor Dinner

"They're probably respectable citizens by this time," broke in Barry.

"Fudge!... Fiddlesticks!"

It was the General's voice, so sudden, so sharp, so rough, we all started. Since the arrival of the telegram he had sat there silent, but apparently this subject was his hobby and it roused him.

"You Americans, sir, believe too much in that sort of thing. You open your doors to the scum and criminals of Europe, and let them overrun the country. Moral regeneration—bah! It's a dangerous principle. Blood is blood! When a man is a traitor and a woman a murderess, the seed of it, I tell you, is in them in their cradles, handed straight down from a former generation. The taint's there and it will stay there, and nothing can change it. You'll learn that in time, in your new country; and you'll do your level best to keep the riffraff out, then, when it's too late. Yes, sir, blood is blood—the children, the children's children unto the third and fourth generation, warped, tainted, mildewed. Why, man, haven't you watched it with the drink curse a score of times?"

Barry started to reply to this rather warmly; then he flushed, hesitated, and looked across at the Doctor. "Of course," he said, "my experience as a lawyer has less to do with blood inheritance

110

The Fourth Generation

than the other kind; and yet I disagree with you. A bruise on an apple does not necessarily spread to the whole apple, unless it is left to rot on the ground. Cut out the bruise with your penknife, and the apple is as good and as sound as ever. But mark you though, this part is imperative, the bruise has got to be cut out. It is America's mission, you may put it her pride, to cut out the bruises that Europe has made; and for that our stock is none the worse." Barry threw back his head and his eyes sparkled.

"Indeed, General, you may not be aware of the fact, but our American apples are justly famous. We supply all your markets, English and otherwise, new species and graftings for all over the world."

A shout of laughter greeted this sally.

General Chatterton frowned. "Bosh!" he retorted, "I was talking of men and you're talking of apples. You lawyers are all alike, all jaw like a sheep's head! You can't remove the moral bruise in a man, more's the pity. The most delicate operation in the world couldn't do it! Ask Ménard here, he's a surgeon, a scientist. It's his field, not ours! ... What do you think of this question, Doctor?"

We all turned and looked at the great man curiously.

The Bachelor Dinner

He was leaning back in his chair with his eyes half closed, his cigar in his mouth, puffing gently; the picture of contentment. Would he talk? Would he rise to the bait or not? There was silence for a moment.

Then Ménard slowly opened one eye and blew a wreath of smoke upward. The rings were perfect; and as they floated, vanished, he watched them lazily.

"Ever know a fellow named Smith, General?" he said.

The Englishman stared at him.

"Really er—I don't know. What was his first name?"

"John."

Ménard puffed out another ring or two.

"Yes, John Smith. That was only his pseudonym, of course. His real name—well, he was pretty famous along his special line. You've all heard of him. Talking of ghost stories! The biggest bogie in the world is heredity, and the only real one. There are precious few men who haven't a skeleton of him, locked up in their closets somewhere. The more respectable the family, the larger the closet room; that's all. But sooner or later he's bound to sneak out.

In the case of—we'll call him J. S. for short—his bogie was a particularly rampant creature. It

The Fourth Generation

came to life first in his great-grandfather's time, and J. S. himself was the fourth generation. Yes, his mother told me the story herself, begged me to help him, begged and implored me. The odds against him were simply appalling. I'll tell you this, gentlemen"—Ménard took the cigar from his mouth and opened the other eye—"I've met a good many men in my day; and the fight some of them have had to make against their own natures, against their own blood as it flows in their veins —it is something more than you ever dreamed of. The marvel is that they ever win out. Yet they do.

You can't get away from heredity, my friends; the General is right there. But conquer and overcome it; cut the bruise out and stop it from spreading, given the will and the pluck to use the scalpel—" the Doctor made a wave of his hand toward Barry—"yes, sir, it happens more times than you think. Take J. S., for example. Here's his experience. A dead secret, needless to say, gentlemen, which is why I use initials. If, by any chance from what I say, you should happen to guess—well, he died only a short time ago, poor fellow; a hero, if ever there was one. To have it known would do him no harm; but on the whole— no. He kept the closet door locked in his life time, and we'll keep it locked now."

The Bachelor Dinner

The Doctor stopped for a moment, flicked the ash from his cigar, settled himself back in his chair and began. By this time Jean had reappeared and the plates had been changed. The sweet and the fruits were already on the table, but no one noticed them; and at a nod from Travis the servant had again withdrawn, closing the door. The smoke in the room was by now like a cloud, out of which the faces around the table rose, interested, eager, bent forward intently.

"The way I first knew of it was this," said Ménard. "The father, old J. S., was a Glasgow merchant, a man well-to-do, honorable, highly respected. He was forty years old when the curse first broke out in him, and it came like a thunderbolt. One night he went to a public dinner. Whether it was that the wines were strong, that he took too much, or merely his condition, that the time for it had come—I don't know. At any rate his wife waited up for him and he never came home. She was nearly crazy.

When J. and I talked over the story years afterward—'That was the first blow my mother had,' he said. She waited for him until four o'clock in the morning, and then she took a cab and went out to search. What possessed her to do it, she said she never knew. She was a woman of some psychic development, and the tie between them had been very strong. The premonition, the instinct to go was irresistible.

The strange part of it was— the part, said J. S., his mother never even tried to explain— she did not go to the club where the dinner was held, or ring up his friends, or do any of the natural things. She took that cab and she drove from dive to dive; places a delicate woman like that could hardly have dreamed of as even existing. Glasgow has plenty of such drinking hells, as any Scotchman can tell you. Well, she drove until she found him. It was still pitch dark, a rainy, sleety December morning. She got him out before the day broke, and back home, under the cover of the mist. Of course no one knew. That was the beginning. After that the thing came on spasmodically, at intervals. In between he was himself. Sometimes months would go by, they'd think he was cured; then in a flash, without any warning, off he would go again.

J. S. said, when he was a little chap his mother always spoke of them as business journeys. 'Your father's away on a business trip,' she'd say, and be as gay and outwardly light-hearted.

Years and years went by. No one ever heard of these early morning cab drives. There wasn't a merchant in Glasgow more respected. No one dreamed of such a thing.

The Bachelor Dinner

There were three sons. The first was a weakling. The curse came on him in his early manhood, and he went under; died of delirium tremens before he'd even started to raise a mustache. The second had better stuff in him and put up a good fight. No one knows just what became of him. He disappeared out of Glasgow one fine morning and was never seen again. Everybody pitied and sympathized with the parents. 'Extraordinary thing!' they said. 'Such a father, such a mother, to have such boys! How on earth could it happen?'

All this time not a breath was ever heard against old J. S. His wife protected him, but she couldn't protect the sons. The dread, the mental racking, during all those years— great heaven, it's awful to think of! She used to pore over books on heredity when the boys were in their cradles, and watch every trait, every instinct, with terror. Nothing did any good. Every year that passed before the outbreak was so much to the good; and that was the only comfort she had. Sooner or later, one son after the other— she never felt safe for one single second. Hell torture is nothing to what that woman went through. J. S. was the third.

The other boys were both gone by that time, and he was a little chap still, when the father died— died in his bed, respectably, peaceably, honorably,

The Fourth Generation

thanks to the woman who stood by him to the end. All the citizens of Glasgow turned out for the funeral, and the funeral oration—" The Doctor threw back his head and laughed grimly.

"Well, poor fellow, poor fellow! If his ghost was still around, it must have had a turn. So thoroughly admired, revered, respected—it was beautiful to listen to. Still never a word, a hint, a breath. The woman had screened him right up to the last, even his memory.

By this time she was still bonny, straight of figure as a girl, but her hair was snow-white. All her love, devotion, care, now centred on her last, her youngest, her baby, her Benjamin. She had lost the other two, she was bound she'd save him. And this is what happened. Gentlemen——"

Ménard flicked the end of his cigar ash off upon his plate. As he went on talking his eyes half closed again, and in between every sentence or two he would stop, blowing a wreath of smoke into the air. "By Christopher! If you guessed who the man was, you would never believe it. But I had the story from his mother, from her own lips; and later still from J. S. himself. It's true, every word.

From the first the boy was an odd little piece, brainy, precocious, stunted in growth, and over-developed mentally; just the temperament for

such a curse to feed on. On it came too, good
and young, and no time lost. In his case however,
strangely enough, instead of the usual signs and
symptoms that the mother knew so well and
watched for, the curse took a different form, a
freak form you might say. He was simply from
the cradle, from the time he took his first steps,
hopelessly, irretrievably, a born vagabond.

J. S. was a toddler when he first made tracks.
A neighbor brought him home. From that time
on he kept the neighbors busy. At seven he ran
away with a gypsy caravan and was gone a whole
year. They advertised, dragged all the ponds in
the neighborhood, gave him up for dead. One day
he walked back. At ten he vanished again for a
while; at fourteen again.

There was nothing to be done, nothing that could
be done in a case like that. Punishment, re-
proaches, appeals to his affection, they were all
tried, they were all alike useless. A word would
move him to tears at the time. He was docile
enough, lovable, penitent, devoted to his mother.
In between, weeks and months would pass, and all
would go right. But when the call came, it was
like a madness, a wild, imperative instinct of the
blood; a call from his inner nature that he could
not control. All of a sudden off he'd go, and wild
horses couldn't hold him.

The Fourth Generation

Things went on this way for some years. Finally one day—as the mother told me afterward, the whole matter was purely accidental—she was in a Glasgow book-shop, and her eye happened to fall on a French monograph. Lehar's famous one, you know, on the treatment of dipsomania, nervous disorders etc., by suggestion; mentioning my name as a specialist in the matter. It was like a straw to a drowning man, she said. Only the week before other symptoms had developed, signs ominous, significant, unmistakable. By then her nerve was all but gone. Her despair had touched bottom. The boy was just turned twenty, clever, gifted, capable of anything; and going to the devil just as fast as he could get there. She clutched the straw with both hands.

What excuse she made to J. S. I never heard exactly, but probably some subterfuge, some subtle, illogical, woman's reason. At any rate she rushed home, packed her bag, sprang her trap. They got away that night, caught the first boat to Calais, and he came like a lamb. One hour after their arrival in Paris she was standing in my office, an utter stranger to me of course. I read her name on the card and I guessed her nationality; otherwise the case was blank. 'What can I do for you, madame?' I said.

She gave me one look; then she flung both hands

to her face and began to— it was worse than mere weeping. I've seen many a woman cry before, but never one like that. There was nothing hysterical. A man might have done it, face to face with some great horror. The tears were tears of blood."

Ménard hesitated, threw away his stub, cut a fresh cigar, lit it, and began to smoke again. He was silent for a little, his eyes half closed, the rings of smoke like a halo above his head. There was a power, a poise about the man even in his relaxation; a certain health-giving, mind-calming atmosphere. We could imagine very well the effect on that woman, the mere knowledge of his presence on emotion such as hers. Before he spoke we knew.

"It was all over in a second," said the Doctor. "With a strong effort of a very strong will, she got herself in hand at once, and began with her story. There was no hesitancy, there was no self pity, there was no side-tracking. She spoke fast and to the point. 'It's the first time in all these years,' she said, 'that I've opened my mouth to a single human being—not to his family, not to mine. Not a soul has ever dreamed. Doctor——'

Her eyes were swollen with weeping, but brave. She looked straight at me. 'Now, at last, I've bared the secret of my heart to you, a heart that's breaking very fast. My boy is at the hotel, wait-

The Fourth Generation

ing for me. He doesn't know I'm here, he thinks'
—she gave a choking laugh—'that I'm at the
Louvre, shopping. Tell me quickly, tell me
frankly, tell me the truth. Is there any hope?'

Gentlemen," said Ménard, "you may not know
it, but if there's any question in the world a doctor
dreads it's that. A mother gazing straight into
your eyes, with the tears welling over, and every
nerve trembling.

'Is there any hope, Doctor? Is there any
hope?'

'Madame,' I said, 'before you ask that question,
I shall have to ask a few myself; and on your answer depends mine. Your husband's father—
what did he die of?'

She began to shake all over.

'And his grandfather? . . . You've studied the
annals, have you?'

She opened her mouth, but not a sound came.

'That's all right,' I said, 'it's just what I supposed. Now, madame, you've done your best to
influence your son, I dare say—you've talked with
him? Have you ever told him the story?'

'Never!' The woman changed in a flash. Her
eyes hardened, her whole body stiffened. 'Blacken
a father's memory to a son? Never in the world!
Rather anything than that. The boys never
guessed, not one of them. When my whole life

The Bachelor Dinner

was one long effort to protect him, shall I tell his
secret now? . . . Never, Doctor! Never!'

In her excitement and wrath she had sprung
to her feet and faced me down; a splendid figure,
tall, regal, with her black veil draped around
her.

'Then—' said I, 'your answer to the first two
questions was of relatively small importance, but
the third settles everything. The case is hopeless.
Good morning, madame.'

'No, Doctor— no, no! I don't understand.
What do you mean?'

'If your son is to put up a fight, madame, you
can't expect him to fight in the dark. He's got to
know what he's fighting against, what his chances
are. The other two went it blind, you say? Well,
you see what happened.'

'You think, Doctor,' she gazed at me, 'if the
other boys had known——'

'I don't say that, madame. The past is the
past, and it can't be helped. What I do say is,
if you send a man out to fight a battle, a battle
for his life, the stronger his equipment, the more
he knows of his enemy's resources, the less the
odds against him. I don't say he'll win, mind,
but at least he starts fair.'

'Must I tell him everything—everything, Doctor? The whole dreadful story, just as——'

The Fourth Generation

'Everything. The whole story, word for word as you told me.'

The woman went over to the window; then she came back, lifted a pamphlet from the table, turned the leaves—put it down again. All the time she saw nothing, she heard nothing, she was struggling. At last—I was watching her—she came to a decision.

'If I do, Doctor— it is terrible to me, it is worse than death. Should a woman be a traitor to her own husband, even to save— If I do, if I do, will you undertake to save him?'

Her whole soul was in her eyes as she asked me this question. She stretched out both her trembling hands, and I took them in mine.

'Go back to your hotel,' I said, 'see your son, tell him everything. And to-morrow morning at nine o'clock send him here to me.'

Her gaze, still imploring, demanded its answer.

'If I do, if I do, will you——'

'Yes, madame,' I said, 'I will undertake to save him.'

Now, gentlemen," said Ménard, "you may think that this was a risky statement, considering statistics. In one sense it was, in another it was not. The toss-up, you see, all depended on one thing—the boy himself. The source of his tastes was only too clear, but from which side came his character? Had he inherited his mother's will or not? On this my treatment hung.

Exactly nine the next morning—the chime of the clock had barely died away when the office bell rang and in walked J. S. That first glimpse of him, that first meeting, I shall always remember. Upon it his whole future life was to swing. This is what I saw.

A frail, undersized fellow, slight of frame and narrow chested, a pack of nerves, and intensely embarrassed. So far his chances were nil. Only two points saved him, only two points in his favor. But on these I staked to win. His eyes were as pure and as frank as a baby's. If any vice was there, it had never rooted deep. And his jaw was like a rock.

This measurement of course was taken in a flash, as the boy crossed the room, as we shook hands together, as he sank back in his chair. No subject this for hypnotic pressure, for leading-strings of any sort, unless so far as suggestion from another will could prick his own to life. J. S. sat there with his head between his hands and stared down at the carpet. From the moment of his entrance he hadn't said a word.

My friends"—Ménard shifted his cigar, a cloud of smoke issuing from his lips as he did so—"there's a canvas in the Gustave Moreau Museum; perhaps

The Fourth Generation

you know it. The subject is 'Hercules and the Dragon of Lerna.' The scene chosen, that where they first meet face to face. There has been no struggle yet, no physical encounter of any sort, not a blow struck either side. Yet the fatal, the critical moment has come. It is this moment— not the battle itself, but the moment before the battle—this is what counted to the painter, and this is what counted to me as the physician. The boy was facing his own lower nature. How would he take it? Would his will recoil from the shock or not? Would it flinch, would it toughen? Was he a weakling, or was he a hero? I studied his profile, bent, pondering; and I thought of that picture.

'Well,' I said, 'how is it? . . . Have you made up your mind?'

He jumped as if he'd been shot.

'What do you mean?' he exclaimed fiercely. 'Don't you know? My mother said she'd told you.'

'Exactly. Sit down, my friend, sit down. Of course she told me. If I hadn't known, I shouldn't have asked you the question. Well?'

J. S. put his hand to his forehead and laughed, a hollow, pathetic laugh. 'Have I made up my mind?' he said. 'Doctor, when a man's tossing and delirious with fever, when a man's raving and mad with a devil inside of him, do you go up to his bedside and ask a thing like that? What do you suppose I've been doing all these years? Fighting, struggling, beating down that devil, sir. I get him down, I get him chained, I get him throttled—just like this, with my hands about his throat. The fiend is finally dead at last, and weeks go by, and months go by; and then all of a sudden——'

The boy's face grew livid, his eyes flashed, his clenched fist struck down with a crash against the desk-top.

'It was just so with my—my father, she tells me! It was just like that with both of my brothers! Great heaven, do you think we're made of stone? That look in my mother's eyes, that heart-rending look of hers, when she sees it coming on! Haven't we all had to face it and go under? Go under in spite of it; in spite of all our struggling, in spite of all our fighting, in spite of everything. You heard, sir, they're dead now; they're gone. Killed by it, choked right off, first one, then the other. I'm the last now. My mother hopes, Doctor, but—you can see it for yourself—I'm tied hand and foot. There isn't any hope.'

He grit his teeth together and looked straight at me squarely.

'Blame me if you like,' he said. 'Call me all the names you choose. Talk religion, talk duty, pour morals down my throat! Oh, I'll sit here, I'll

The Fourth Generation

listen. I've heard it all before. When you get through, you won't have said a single word that I haven't said to myself a hundred times, a thousand times, a million times. Has it done any good? My God! My God! You don't know what it is! You don't know what you're talking about!' He sprang to his feet and began pacing the room.

'Young man,' I said, 'I'm a physician, not a clergyman. Your religion and morals are not my affair.'

J. S. stopped. A relieved look flashed over his face for a moment; then the dogged, sullen lines settled again about his mouth.

'No, no,' he muttered, 'of course not. I might have known. A cure then, Doctor; is that what you're after? Oh, for heaven's sake, don't! I've gone through enough of that fool sort of business. It's all poppycock!' Again he gave that hollow laugh that chilled my very blood.

'I tell you, sir, believe me or not—when that wandering devil of mine wakes up, when the fit once takes hold, the instinct to make tracks, to break loose, to jump the halter, it's like a magnet drawing me off and away. Against reason, against conscience, against common-sense, to hell with all convention! When the moment comes that's the feeling, explain it as you may, and there's no living power on earth that can stop me.'

The Bachelor Dinner

'No,' said I, 'of course not. If I were you I shouldn't try.'

'Not try?' exclaimed J. S.

The boy was so surprised that he stood stock-still staring.

'When a fire is out of control, my friend, never try to smother it. If the flames are underneath there, red-hot, smouldering, suppress them in one place and they'll break out in another. Bound to, you see, and worse and worse every time. Now there are only two ways of dealing with a fire. Put it out if you can. If you can't, why give it the safest outlet.'

He nodded at me blankly.

'The safest outlet for you, J. S., is to pull up your tent-stakes. Double-quick too before—— '

Again he nodded, but a brighter look came into his eyes, almost a ray of hope.

'Yes,' said I, 'you understand? . . . I had a horse once that always ran away. He would do it. Probably had a sire, or a grandsire, or something. Well, I let him run, I had to, but I kept him in the road. It was hard work pulling, and it almost broke my wrists; but that much we settled at the start. No shies, no swerves, no smashing up the curb. If he ran, he ran straight. In the end he proved a first-class horse, one of the best I ever had.'

The Fourth Generation

'You mean—' he stammered. The ray of hope was widening.

'You've got a strong instinct, my friend. Well, follow it. Follow it up and follow it closely. Make yourself a specialist along those certain lines, whatever they are! Work like the devil; and control the rest. My prophecy is——'

'What?' he cried. 'What?'

The boy was still on his feet, but his attitude had changed. He was tense, erect, eager, like a young hound when there's scent in the wind, tugging, straining, before you slip the leash.

'Ten years from now you'll be somebody,' I said, 'just what I can't tell. Your road will be a hard one, harder than most because it's off the beaten track. You'll have to blaze your own trail, uproot your own snags; and the world will be against you. But you've pluck, you've talent, you've a will of fine steel, and you're bound to win out. Remember that. No matter what happens, no matter how you seem to fail—you're bound to win out.'

Gentlemen—" said Ménard. He stopped and struck a match, stooping over for a moment. "When I said that, I looked that young fellow straight in the eyes. His gaze came back to me steady, unblinking.

'In spite of my inheritance, Doctor?'

'In spite of your inheritance.'

129

The Bachelor Dinner

'You believe in me?'

'I do.'

'You think—you really think that I have a career before me, like other men? That I can——'

'Certainly. Why not?'

'That I shan't end like—like the others, and break my mother's heart?'

'Never! Never in the world!'

'What—what about her, Doctor?'

'You leave your mother to me, J. S. You're doing it for her, aren't you? She'll understand; she's a wonderful woman, and it's lucky for you that you've got her inside of you. Be off now, be off! You only have ten years.'

The boy flung one look at me, a grasp of the hand; then the door slammed behind him. I could hear his feet on the stairway outside, running, jumping, four steps at a time." Ménard gave a little laugh.

"That interview with J. S.," he said, "it lasted barely half an hour, but it was the best morning's work of my whole life, gentlemen."

"What happened, Doctor?"

It was Barry who put the question, but the exclamations went like a chorus around the table.

"Yes, Doctor—what became of him?"

"What happened! What became of him!" Ménard repeated the words with emphasis.

The Fourth Generation

"Why the boy sailed the next morning, sailed to
America. Went on the North German Lloyd as
a stoker, worked his way across. Wouldn't ask
his mother for a penny, she told me. Just
rushed in, kissed her good-by, referred her to
me for explanation, and was away like a flash.
Just the old story over again, she thought in her
despair.

But it wasn't. It was different.

For ten years that fellow tramped the earth.
He went everywhere, he saw everything. What he
must have gone through with that devil of his,
no one ever heard exactly; but his resource and
his vitality were alike boundless. He found he
couldn't kill his dragon, so he tamed it to his will.
And he got to know the underworld, the shifting,
seething flotsam and jetsam of life, the wrecks, the
freaks, the class beyond the pale, as no other
human being has ever known it before. At twenty-
five already his articles were talked about. At
thirty he was recognized as an authority on the
subject. Sociologists went to him for advice, and
criminologists came to ask his opinion. He knew,
you see. The germs of it were all within himself.
He spoke from the inside; and the rest were, and
always would be, amateurs, outsiders. Yes, in
ten years J. S.—it was just as I told him. His
mother lived to see him famous."

The Bachelor Dinner

"Was it hypnotism, Doctor?"

Barry started suddenly and leaned forward. "What? No! . . . You kept in touch with him all that time, you had him under control, did you? By Jove, sir, that's interesting!"

We all stared excitedly over at Ménard. His face was impassive.

"Oh, no," he said, "no! . . . The cigars, thank you, Travis! . . . Call it hypnotism if you like, call it suggestion, call it a knowledge of human nature. Call it anything you choose. My part in the matter was perfectly simple. Diagnosis and prescription. J. S. did the rest himself.

That is the history of his bogie, gentlemen. When he died a year ago, every newspaper in the country had a column on his tramp-life, on his research-work, his character, his honors. He deserved it too, every word. But the bogie wasn't mentioned. The real reason for that life of his, those ten long years of battle that made him what he was—the facts were never known at all. You see, gentlemen, by this case, what the scalpel can accomplish even"— Ménard turned and gave a nod toward Barry—"even when it comes to the Fourth Generation!"

"Yes, yes, the fourth!" exclaimed the General, "the fourth! That's all very well, sir! Very plausible indeed. But what about the fifth?

The Fourth Generation

That's what I want to know. Did the curse re-appear? What about the——"

The Doctor went on smoking for a moment in silence, his head back, his eyes half closed. He seemed to be pondering.

"Eh?... What about the fifth, Doctor?"

"That we'll never know," he said slowly. "Thank God, there wasn't any!"

Mademoiselle Mimi

THERE was a moment of stillness about the circle; and then Barry took a mandarin from the fruit plate and began to peel it, scenting the fragrant skin as he did so.

"Like a whiff of the South," he remarked thoughtfully. "Never see them or smell them that they don't take me back to Italy! Curious thing that, Doctor. How little one really knows of the lives of some of these famous people! Biographies, autobiographies, letters, diaries—bah! They tell what they like, turn a certain front to the world with a searchlight on it, and the rest is blank; a mystery impenetrable as the ocean in a fog. The real truth—I suppose that's so about most of us—it links the lies together like the key-stone of an arch. If one could only dislodge it!"

"If you did, you would get the surprise of your life," said the Doctor, "and just for that reason it's never safe to meddle. The mysteries of bridge construction are as a-b-c, in comparison to the inner workings of a human being. I never run across a new personality, a strong, distinctive, odd one apart from the type, a man or woman or child

of mark, a talent, a genius, that I don't rack my
brains wondering what lies behind the veil. Of
course, a doctor's field is limited. He's apt to
meet the maimed ones, off somewhere either in
mind or body, abnormal for the time and not themselves. Otherwise they wouldn't seek him. Once
a bird's wings are mended, its eyes bright, its poise
and confidence restored, off it flies! As a matter of
fact, the doctor sees the bird down, but he rarely
sees it flying. Now with you, monsieur"—the
Doctor turned suddenly and looked straight at
Taglioni—"in your profession, I take it, it's just
the other way."

The Italian started slightly.

All through the dinner, up to now, he had sat
very silent, listening to the others. A short man
with a strange, big head; the hair worn long like a
musician's, thick and grizzled, the mouth finely
moulded; the rest of the face rather coarse, bat-
tered as if from overmuch living, an impression
that vanished as soon as he spoke. His response to
Ménard's question was so spontaneous, his smile
so childlike, so disarming, that his whole aspect
changed, grew refined in a flash. A chevalier in
manner like most Italians, the spell of it affected
us like a perfume in the room.

"Ah, the song-birds—sì? You have interest
in them, signore, you would hear their secrets?"

The Bachelor Dinner

He laughed out gayly. "It is true what you say. The public knows nothing, the reporters know nothing, the other artists, even they know nothing. Only the maid knows sometimes, if it is a good maid, a faithful maid; and the impresario occasionally when, if— Yes, I have heard things!"

Taglioni stretched out his hand to Barry's plate and took a strip of the mandarin peel, holding it up to his face, crushing it between his fingers.

"Permit me, signore. A very beautiful aroma, just as you said. It reminds one of so much— blue seas, bright skies, a terrace, a garden, flowers, moonlight—all that is subtle, seductive, sensuous! . . . Have you ever heard of Mademoiselle Mimi?"

"A singer?" questioned Ménard.

"Yes, signore, a singer, a prima donna. One of the greatest on the stage to-day. She sings everywhere—Milan, Paris, Covent Garden, the Metropolitan—a voice like a flute and a 'cello rolled in one. If you go to opera anywhere you must have heard her sing."

"Mademoiselle Mimi? . . . No. Never heard the name."

Barry shook his head and frowned; the Doctor shrugged his shoulders.

"Strange," said Taglioni. "Whenever I touch a mandarin it makes me think of her. It makes me think of that night on Como, that night on the terrace when the moon was creeping up. She wasn't a prima donna then; she hadn't been discovered. Ever heard of Carmen, or Tosca, or Zaza?"

We all burst out laughing and stared at Taglioni.

"Well," he said, "she's been them all turn and turn about; those and hosts of others. But behind the footlights—this is a greenroom secret, gentlemen, so please don't divulge it—*La Bohème*, that was her first great part, the part that made her famous. Since then, among her friends, her intimates, those who know and love her best, she goes always by the pet name of Mademoiselle Mimi."

"What's her real name?" said Barry.

Taglioni looked around and put his finger to his lips.

"An impresario has many an adventure, signore. In dealing with artists the nerves must be of steel, the tongue must be of velvet. Any moment things may happen; even at the last hour, with the box office sold out and the singers in their dressing-rooms waiting for the call bell. It may be jealousy, it may be temper, a little misunderstanding; or it may be laryngitis. One never knows. Sometimes it is only the fire-curtain that insists on coming down just when it shouldn't.

The Bachelor Dinner

Sometimes the ballet-dancers all go on a strike. Once a tenor went stark mad in the middle of an aria and transposed all his notes. We lured him off the stage with difficulty, telephoned a hurry call for his understudy; and the opera went on. Once the Carmen cracked her voice—lost it right out of her throat, signore, at the last F$^\sharp$ of the Habañera—all of a sudden went hoarse as a crow and flatted like a church bell!... Yes, signore, an impresario—he must have the soft tongue, the quick eye, the steady heart; otherwise he dies young."

Taglioni smoothed the mandarin peel caressingly, and tossed back a stray heavy lock of his hair, "*Diavolo*, signore! A curious fact, but true! It was the crack in that soprano—you may not believe it—that sent me to Como in May, to Tremezzo. And that's how and where——"

He stopped and gave a gay laugh.

"In those days the strain was great and the pulse was not so steady. It was Saturday night that the Carmen went smash. I dropped my head in my hands like this; tore my hair, stamped my foot, rushed around, telegraphed, telephoned—turned the world upsidedown. The season had been unlucky all along the line. One soprano in the doctor's hands. Another also in the doctor's hands. A third— same place! What was I to do?

138

Mademoiselle Mimi

You can't give grand opera, you can't give opera comique, opera bouffe, opera anything with that sort of a cast! A crack in the upper register six notes across! *Per Dio!* And the theatre full up for *Traviata* Monday night!"

"Great Scott!" exclaimed Barry. "I should think you would die young! Worse than being a lawyer. Did you call in the tickets, sir, and close the house, or what?"

Taglioni lifted one shoulder and made a gesture with both hands; a rapid negative, scorn-expressing gesture.

"No," he said, "of course not! There's never a labyrinth so winding that there isn't some way out. I took the first train to Como to interview Marczala. Better a setting star than no star at all. She was living there, retired, at her villa near Tremezzo. A kind heart, past the years, but a voice still on the pitch. A little flattery, a little tact, a little coaxing— she'd do it. It was dusk when I arrived."

Taglioni looked down at the twisted peel in his hand, unfolded it gently and then curled it up again.

"Yes, a May evening, soft, balmy. The magnolias were in bloom, the terrace was in shadow, the moon was just rising above the mountains of Lecco. After the rush and din of Milan the stillness was enchanting, the scented air a sleeping potion to the overtaxed nerves. I lit a cigarette and strolled out along the lake-side. My meeting with Marczala was due at ten o'clock. Until then she was engaged with guests, and until then I was free. Signori"—Taglioni drew a long breath as if drawing in some fragrance—"you know our lakes in May? It is then one thanks God to be an Italian, to be alive in such a world!

It was just under the trees by the Villa Carlotta; there beyond the steps, where the wall curves out. All of a sudden I stopped lazily, languidly, and leaned against the wall. The path was blocked. A small crowd of hotel guests from the neighborhood, also lazy, also languid, were grouped about in a circle, mingling with the natives. From the centre—it is always so on a moonlight night in Italy—came the glint of color, the sound of singing, the twanging of guitar strings.

Mademoiselle Mimi

Any evening, in any village all along the lakeside, from Lenno to Cadenabbia you can hear the same thing. So then," Taglioni laughed, "since I could not go on, since I would not go back, there was nothing else to do but light another cigarette, lean against the wall, watch the splashing of the water, the gay-garbed troupe, and listen.

There were five musicians in all. One played the mandolin, one played the guitar, two played violins, and the fifth had castanets. Three were men and two were girls. From their dialect, their looks, the way they flashed their teeth and laughed, with that inborn, infectious, irresponsible abandon of the South, it was easy enough to see that the troupe was Neapolitan. One girl in particular caught my eye at once.

She was the darkest of the lot. Hair and eyes black as sloes; a face oval, olive-tinted, with the rich blood near the surface; brows straight and eyelashes that curled up and tangled; the reddest lips you ever saw, and a form as graceful, as slender as a Psyche. Her skirt was dull blue, faded. Around her shoulders was a crimson scarf with tassels. In her hair was thrust a rose, and from her ears hung ear-rings. She was standing a little apart from the others, her dark head tipped sideways, shaking the castanets, clicking them in rhythm with the music.

141

The Bachelor Dinner

Apart from her beauty, apart from any grace of poise, there was something in that street girl, something inexplicable, indescribable, that arrested the attention of everybody there. The man with the guitar was in front singing, but no one noticed him. The other woman was pretty enough, bright-eyed, full of dash. No one gave her a glance. Now, signore—" Taglioni turned to Barry.

"If you go much to the theatre, if you know about the stage, there is one point that may or may not have proved an enigma. It is to most laymen who take interest in the footlights. It is even to the impresarios. We recognize, we use the secret; but we never make any attempt at explanation. What is it that holds the public? It isn't beauty. A woman may be as handsome as a Juno and be a dead failure. It isn't voice or training. There are scores of good voices that never leave the chorus. It isn't acting alone, and it isn't mere talent. What is this subtle something, signore? How can you explain it?"

"I don't know," said Barry, thoughtfully. "The first time I saw Duse— it was before the rest of the world knew anything about her, before she'd been advertised, before she was anybody. One night I was passing a theatre with a friend. A heavy storm had just come up and we dropped

142

inside for shelter. What the play was we didn't know; who the actors were we didn't care. It was a travelling company, and we too were travellers; in there to keep dry, for no other reason. It was pitch dark in the house when we entered, and the curtain was up. The first act had just begun. Already several of the company were on the stage talking. We yawned and glanced around us. The theatre was large, black, empty. Besides ourselves not a dozen in the audience, all told. By Jove! We looked at one another, laughed, and glanced back at the stage.

In the background of the scene, half in shadow, was a flight of steps; crouched on the steps a figure. A drab-colored cloak, a hood over the head, the face turned and hidden. The light was so dim, one had to strain to make it out at all; but once those steps were located, our gaze remained fixed. The figure never stirred. What there was, I couldn't tell you. Everything was focussed for the other side of the stage, but not one of those present even glanced there or listened. We watched that crouching figure, that shrouded, motionless, mysterious woman's figure; and we all but held our breath. It was like some hypnotic influence, a force impossible to fathom, so intense, so subtle, so grasping and illusive. Not a soul could look away.

143

The Bachelor Dinner

When the figure rose from the steps at last—
Well, gentlemen, that was Duse! That was how
she made her entrance! As the play went on no
one else existed; the rest were marionettes. She
twisted our emotions all around her little finger.
She held those twelve people in the hollow of her
hand. At the end—a dozen throats, a dozen pair
of hands—yet they cheered her to the echo, they
made the roof ring!

The next night we went again; the house was
half full. The next— packed, jammed, not a seat
for love or money. After that— you know the
rest! A strange, a marvellous power, yes, sir!"
Barry nodded to Taglioni. "Those who have
it are few; but when they do—" he laughed.
"Is that how you stumbled on Mademoiselle
Mimi?"

"Just so!" exclaimed Taglioni. "Just exactly
so, signore! That night by the lake-side— she was
nothing yet; she was nobody at all! The girl
simply stood there, swaying to the music, flashing
her lips and her eyes at the crowd, clicking with
the castanets. The others did the playing and the
singing and the work. The people watched her.
Ha! ha! ha! This was the thought that came to
my mind: 'If that little devil of a Neapolitan
passes the plate, the copper, the silver will fall
into it like rain! With a personality as vivid, as

vibrant as hers, she will never go hungry. Her share of bread is more than earned if she never opens her mouth.' And then all of a sudden, even as I thought it, the instruments began to play again gayly, mockingly, a Neapolitan love song; and the girl sprang forward.

That moment, signore—" Taglioni hesitated, "it was the one that counted most in my whole career as impresario. I shall never forget it, and neither will she. The song was common enough. Just a simple air.

A thousand times you must have heard it if you've ever been in Naples. But how she sang it! *Dio mio!* No one, not even the Neapolitans themselves, ever heard it sung like that!

Her voice was pure as crystal, and every tone reflected back a dozen shades of feeling, your own, her own, the others—the moods of wandering, loneliness, ecstatic joy, abandon—moonlight, fragrance, the scent of oleanders, the splashing of the water. Just as the colors of the kaleidoscope mingle and fall and are never still an instant, so the emotions were shaken, thrilled, played on. And as she sang she danced. The dusk of her skin was soft like a rose-leaf, her red lips parted, her dark eyes shone. One arm was curved above her head, clicking the castanets in rhythm to the music. Her feet tapped the pebbles; her slim body swayed. *Diavolo!*"

Taglioni was silent for a moment, twisting the mandarin peel absent-mindedly in and out between his fingers.

"Yes, signori, that is how it was. The people went quite mad. They clapped and stamped and made as much noise as the Dal Verme packed on a popular night—and all for a street singer, if you please, a Neapolitan! She curtsied and laughed like a pleased child, and the instruments began again. I could hardly believe my ears, for all it is such a favorite always with the wandering singers. They began Carmen's love song. Yes, that very Habañera! The girl curved her arms again and clicked the castanets, half closing her eyes.

You remember how it goes? Four bars pizzicato with the strings, and then the voice.

Mademoiselle Mimi

She started in dreamily, seductively, piano; veiling the tones, breathing out the sound. The passion of the wild thing, half revealed, half restrained; the instinct for something beyond, it knows not what. With the repetition of the theme the voice grew fuller, less pathetic, more intense, vibrating, defiant. Where the key changes to the two sharps—you recall it?—all of a sudden the tempo quickened, the castanets clicked with more deviltry, abandon. Passion woke up and caught the senses in its leash. The voice soared, swelled. The instruments ran riot, pizzicato, pizzicato, right up to that last long $F^\sharp$ and drop, that left us startled, breathless, staring a moment, still under the spell.

That Habañera, signore, I had heard it all my life—all the Carmens, one after the other, at the

The Bachelor Dinner

Dal Verme, at the Scala; and there I stood speech-
less, taken off my feet as any country gawk at his
first entrance to the gallery. *Madonna!* How
they clapped, how they stamped, how they roared!
The crowd had swelled by this time under the trees.
The boat-steps, the wall, the terrace, all were
crowded. Of course long before, I had made up
my mind. But how to get hold of the girl to talk
with her, that was the question—to penetrate beyond the throng! I glanced uneasily around. Was
any other impresario by chance on the ground, or
was I the first?

Ah, in those days, signori, the pulses beat
quickly just as I told you, the heart was eager.
When I heard that Habañera I knew my name
was made. Again I glanced around. The musicians were resting, chatting together, tuning up
their instruments. In and out amongst the crowd,
a shimmer of dull blue, a glitter of ear-rings, a
rose peeping out of a dusky cloud of hair—the
singer with her red lips smiling, parted, was hand-
ing around the tambourine. The click of the coppers fell into it like hail. I stood with my hands
in my pockets, listening, watching the movement
and excitement of the crowd. The coppers rattled
louder, and the girl came nearer.

When she was near enough, close behind my
shoulder, I turned and confronted her sharply,

148

Mademoiselle Mimi

face to face. She held up the tambourine and her black eyes flashed to mine. *Diavolo*, signore! With all the laughter in them, there was something more behind it, a dignity, a poise, a pride of will and bearing. No prima donna could have equalled it at a thousand francs a night! I dropped my coppers humbly.

'May I speak with you?' I said.

'What about?' Her tone was haughty.

'About yourself.'

'No.'

'About your voice, signorina.'

She glanced at me over her shoulder and hesitated.

'Who are you, signore?'

'An impresario from Milan.'

'Ah!' She hesitated again, half turned and regarded me steadily. 'If it is about my voice then, *la voce mia*—meet me at ten o'clock here by the wall. The crowd will have melted by that time. *Addio!*'

She vanished through the throng.

That night"—Taglioni gave a laugh—"two engagements with artists at the same hour, a prima donna and a street singer. A devil of a hole for a poor impresario! But the strangest part about it was——"

"What?" we all exclaimed.

The Bachelor Dinner

"Wait," he said; "wait until I tell you the story, just as she told it to me, word for word. If the world should get to hear it, if the public ever knew!... Well, ten o'clock struck. I had sent a message to Marczala meanwhile: 'Unavoidably detained. Will see you in the morning.' And there I stood in the shadow of the wall, waiting, impatient. The musicians were gone; the crowd had disappeared. The night was silent and still and fragrant. Across the water lay a white trail of moonlight. Would the girl come or not?

Just as I was taking my watch from my pocket two figures came hastily, the only ones in sight, along the path from Cadenabbia. Skirting the boat-steps they hurried straight toward me. The singer was ahead. She whispered to her companion, who stopped where she was; and then the girl with the rose in her hair came forward alone, the little Neapolitan."

Taglioni laughed again. "Yes, signori," he said, "that was Mademoiselle Mimi. She began humbly enough, you must admit. And that night by the lake-side she signed her first contract. I had it all made out. A simple enough little sheet when you think what she is now.

'Read it through,' I said, 'here by the light of the moon, and sign your name below.'

It was then the real truth came out.

Mademoiselle Mimi

'My name?' the girl repeated. She was stammering suddenly, and her face was like a sheet.

'Of course! Your full name here.'

I handed her my fountain-pen; and she turned her shoulder to me, bending down against the wall. She could not write perhaps? With these Neapolitan singers it is often that way. The girl stared down at the paper, shivering. It rustled between her fingers.

'No, no,' she cried, 'it's not that!' divining my thought. 'Hush, signore, come nearer; I will tell you my secret. But first, swear——'

Then hurriedly, with flashing eyes, she told me who she was. You will never believe it, gentlemen, but the story is a fact. One of those strange mysteries that are disclosed, if ever, to a future generation, seldom to our own. . . . Sir, do you believe in international marriages?"

The question put to Barry was so curt, so unexpected, that the knife he was holding dropped from his fingers, and he stared at the Italian blankly, in amazement. "I?" he said. "Why, no, I don't! But what the deuce——"

Taglioni waved his hand.

"A pity," he said, "these beautiful American signorine, they do not think the same! So many tragedies and dramas would be avoided. The fortune weighs in the scale one end, the title in

The Bachelor Dinner

the other. A thousand pities, yes! For instance, the marriage of the Marchese della— A great name in Italy, gentlemen, too great to mention. He wasn't much except for that. He had a palace in Rome, and a half-ruined castle up in the Abruzzi; and his creditors stretched all the way from the Corso to the cemetery. It was because of them that he went to America. In fact he was obliged to; his family sent him. A friend of his had just gone out a few months before, and had come back successful. His errand was the same."

"Also successful?" demanded Barry dryly.

"Quite so," said Taglioni, "oh, eminently so! The bride was very pretty, very charming, very— well, everything he could have asked."

"Of course," exclaimed Barry, "of course! Excuse me for interrupting your story, monsieur; but this subject of international marriage, since you ask me—by Jove! I could tell you things about it that would open your eyes. I've been looking into this very matter lately. Indeed the fact is, that is what I'm here for now. My client— this of course is secret, gentlemen; it's a case just in point. An American girl, young, ambitious, romantic, knowing as much or as little about the foreign world as a two-year-old baby; married six months to a French count, who is making ducks and drakes of her fortune. Ducks and drakes of

Mademoiselle Mimi

her heart too for that matter! As soon as I can settle the divorce she's going back. What on earth makes them do it?"

Barry brought his fist with a crash down on the table. "Every year another victim, another knot tied! Miss Mary Ann Brown becomes la Principessa Anna Maria di Brunetti! Lohengrin, orange-blossoms, white satin, wedding-cake, and silver tinsel—all the rest. Presto! change! Very easy, very simple. A few dozen words from the minister, and it's finished. But when the knot is ravelled and you want to untie it, when we lawyers come in—to transpose the Principessa Anna Maria di Brunetti back to plain Mary Ann Brown again— well, it's a hell of a job!" said Barry. "The first time I ran across it——"

Taglioni took another strip of mandarin, and balanced it thoughtfully across his little finger. "Yes?" he said. "Go on, signore."

"Why, it was back in my own native State," my friend continued, "down in old Virginia. Our old Judge there—he was one of the finest types of men you ever saw, the type of Southern gentleman that's fast dying out—stern, chivalrous, cultured, a Galahad in honor, a very king on his own plantation. A thousand straight acres of tobacco fields growing, a small army of darkies to raise it, who both adored and feared him; and a homestead

153

more beautiful than any English manor. He kept
open house there all the year round—hospitality
with both hands out, so to speak.

His daughters were the belles of Virginia in their
day. When they went up to Washington for the
dances in the season, they were always known as
the beautiful sisters. Very dark, both of them;
curly hair, great black eyes, cheeks and lips as red
as health could paint them, and skin like tinted
ivory. Petite, graceful, splendid horse-women—
dance half the night and be off at daybreak in the
saddle—that sort of girls, full of life and vim and
energy.

The eldest—it was an awful blow to the old
Judge when it happened—she was engaged, before
her first season was half-way over, to a titled good-
for-nothing, a Duca della something-or-other. I
forget his name now. Well, the girl was very pretty, very determined, very much in love. American, she was used to carrying all before her; and she
got her own way! She married in spite of opposition. The wedding was one of the events of society, an international affair. The groom was in
uniform, sky blue and gold and all sorts of fandan-
gos, best man, etc., imported from Italy—and so
the thing went off. The couple sailed away."

Barry looked over at Taglioni and hesitated,
"You don't mind," he said, "if——"

Mademoiselle Mimi

The Italian shrugged his shoulders. "The fact's well known," he said, "over here. The Old World has no illusions in regard to its so-called aristocracy. It's only you Americans who persist in your idealism, who walk into it blindfold. What happened, signore?"

He spoke carelessly, still toying with the mandarin, arranging the peel in little strips around his plate.

"I don't know," said Barry, "no one ever knew. It was a queer business altogether. The wedding was at Easter. In June the bride returned. All the gay color was gone from her cheeks, all the youth from her bearing. She looked years older, wan-eyed, delicate, like a frail white anemone nipped by the frost. She came back alone. The ostensible reason—and this was the queerest part of all—she came back to be present at her younger sister's wedding. Another international marriage, if you please! An Italian Marchese, and her husband's best man of three months before. But the Duca della something-or-other himself, whatever it was—his pale young Duchessa had to make excuses for him. 'He was ill, he was busy, detained by his estates, summoned for army manœuvres,' etc.

She said it with a smile, a straightening of the shoulders, a faint replica of the old gay spirit. Of

The Bachelor Dinner

course the world talked, the world wondered. What was the old Judge about to allow it? Another daughter, his youngest, his darling—with the consequences of the first mistake right before his eyes! But whatever happened there, the family was proud, and they kept things to themselves. A strange wedding, that!

On the surface everything festive, delightful; clear skies and a full surpliced choir. Underneath, it was like a minor chord sustained, scarcely sounding; a hint of past battle, of coming storm and tragedy. As the wedding procession advanced toward the altar, I shall never forget that strange tense impression. The old Judge, grim, dark-browed, silent; the bride on his arm young, radiant, gazing happy-hearted, whole-souled straight ahead of her. No doubt or fear there! Beyond, the Marchese, his face averted, waiting. All about the throng of guests. In every mind a question.

The answer to that question, gentlemen? Well, it leaked out years afterward, somehow, somewhere; accidentally, as most secrets do sooner or later. A servant, a relation, somebody whispered. A whisper overheard, repeated, enlarged on. The scene in that family just before the wedding, they said, had been beyond words!

On the one side the old Judge, who was dead set

against it, and had a will of iron; with him the
Duchessa, who had come back for no other purpose, who warned and pleaded with her sister on
her knees. Even the old aunt, who had mothered
the girls since their babyhood; who had spoiled,
adored, given in to them always. The three
stood solid. And against that phalanx a mere
slip of a girl, scarcely out of her teens. A gay,
self-willed child, whose path in life so far had
been hedged about with roses; who having seen
only roses and never felt a thorn, dreamed from
past experience of more roses just ahead. All
they did, all they said— it was like trying to
reason with a swallow that had never flown before. The sky was blue, the air was sweet, the
wings were strong and fluttering. All the world
before it; and the cat below was hidden.

One after the other, first the aunt, then the
Duchessa, gave up in despair. At last only the
old Judge was left, still determined, inexorable.
The sharpest weapon in his hand, the only one in
such a case, lay shattered, useless in his grasp. The
girl had inherited her fortune from her mother.

She was of age; and this was the strangest part
of all. Whether influenced by the Marchese or
maddened by the long fight and the aspersions cast
against him, the loyalty of the girl was aroused,
who can tell? But this is a fact, and I know it

The Bachelor Dinner

from her lawyers. The day before the wedding she made her entire fortune over, every stock, every bond, every investment, every dollar, to the man whom she trusted and loved—to her husband.

It was then the storm broke. The Judge, they said, was white with passion, petrified with horror. When he learned, it was too late. The papers were made out, ready, waiting to be signed, in his daughter's hand.

'If you do,' he said, 'if you do, remember this. From the moment that you leave my house, from the moment that the clock strikes to-morrow at noon, you will have to bear the consequences, whatever they are! Whatever they are, do you understand? One daughter has come home to me, crushed and broken, her heart's blood drained by these accursed foreigners! In her case there was some excuse, in spite of my misgivings. She went into it ignorant, innocent, unwarned. In your case there is none. This man is a friend of the other, here for the same purpose—not for you, but for what you can give him; as much a beggar and more than the tramp who comes whining to the back kitchen door.

'To go through this thing a second time—the strain, the shock, the humiliation—it would kill your aunt, it would kill your sister; and I tell you frankly for myself I couldn't bear it. You will have to choose now, to-day, this moment. Either tear those papers up, send the beggar about his business; or go ahead, face the consequences, and keep quiet about it! . . . Will you sign or not?'

The girl took the papers over to the desk without a word, dipped the pen into the ink and wrote her name across them, one after the other. A hand firm and round and clear, without a trace of trembling.

That was all," said Barry. "The wedding went off, just as I told you. She kissed her family good-by, and the last they saw of her she was leaning forward in the carriage beside the Marchese, waving her hand, smiling, radiant, while the rice showered in on them from all sides like snowflakes. And then the carriage vanished."

"Well?" said Taglioni.

"Well," said Barry, "curiously enough— you'll be surprised, I daresay, but it turned out all right. At least as far as any one ever heard to the contrary. She used to write home regularly once a month or so. I think she does still; but the old Judge, the aunt, the Duchessa—they never came abroad. In fact, after that, they seldom left Virginia; and the Marchesa never returned. She lived in Italy with her husband. As the years went by— you know how such things are. Her friends at home lost track of her shortly after marriage. They said she was exclusive, proud of her title, only cared for the nobility, was weaned entirely away from America. Whether that was true or not, at any rate her letters to the family were gay, affectionate, rosy-hued always.

Oh yes, it turned out well. For once the Judge —a keen old chap too he was for reading character, but this once he proved wrong. The last news I had was several years ago. The family were still down on the plantation in Virginia; and the Marchesa was living in one of her castles somewhere in Italy—living rather retired because of ill health, but always very happy and contented with her husband.

Yes," said Barry, calculating, "so far as my experience goes, that's the one international marriage that was lucky, the only one that I can think of where it did turn out all right. But— I beg your pardon, sir!"

He looked up suddenly and met Taglioni's eye.

"I didn't mean to interrupt you, monsieur. You were saying——"

"Oh, nothing," said Taglioni, "nothing! You mean about the singer?"

"Why, the little Neapolitan," we all exclaimed, "Mademoiselle Mimi! Who was she really, your great prima donna? You were just about to tell us."

Mademoiselle Mimi

The Italian shrugged his shoulders.

"Oh, nobody," he said, "nobody in particular. Just a girl who had married a man high up in the world as to name, and nowhere at all as to achievements and character. A mistake like hosts of others. And she found him out, that's all. When she did—this is really the odd part about it, signori, and what set the girl, for me, apart from other women. She was too proud to go on living with a man of that sort; she was too proud also to let the world suspect. Besides there were reasons. So one day they had a frank talk; and the next in all the *giornali di Roma* it was stated that so-and-so, for reasons of health, had retired to her castle up in the Abruzzi. There she has been ever since, and there she is to-day. Any one in Rome will tell you. The husband— well, he hunts, or yachts, or loafs around the Corso, drinks vermouth at Aragno's, drives a brake up on the Pincio. I've seen him many a time. He does it all on his wife's money."

"You mean to say—" cried Barry. "What?"

"Pisht!" Taglioni waved his hand. "That castle in the Abruzzi is as empty as your hand. A half-ruined, deserted tomb of a place, where the bats fly in and out. But it saved the situation. As an alibi the wife is there. In reality she vanished, leaving her good name and her worldly

The Bachelor Dinner

goods behind her. That was the bargain. She vanished completely, body, soul, and spirit, off the earth and has never been seen from that day to this! . . . What became of her, signore— if you ask me that question!"

Taglioni gazed down at his plate, at the little strips of mandarin peel, and shifted them about, absently, carelessly, as if his mind were far away.

"*Dio!* Luckily she had pluck, a grand talent, and a Neapolitan maid—a devoted, faithful soul, who taught her the dialect, showed her how to act the part, and stuck to her through thick and thin. That is how it happened. She told me the story herself, there by the wall, that soft evening in the moonlight; and then she signed her married name. But first she made me swear—" Taglioni nodded slowly.

"There's no better disguise than grand opera," he said. "She has kept it all these years, in Italy, in France, in England, in America. Not a soul has ever dreamed."

Barry put his hand to his forehead suddenly as if a thought had struck him. "No, no," he cried, "she couldn't be! Impossible! The maiden name, the nationality, monsieur— did she tell you?"

The impresario hesitated; then he glanced around the table.

Mademoiselle Mimi

"*Chi lo sa!* . . . Perhaps she did, perhaps she didn't! My memory for such things is so very poor, signore. And besides, what does it matter? I was in a church once in Rome, a high pontifical mass at S. Carlo in Corso, and the bishop who officiated, he was darker even than most Italians; and he wore the triple hat in gold, the purple robes, the lace cotta, buckled shoes, all the fixings, surrounded by acolytes, priests, candles. The occasion was some special one and the nave was filled with tourists. An American girl was standing at my elbow.

'What a Roman scene!' she said, 'and that bishop—how Italian!'

As a matter of fact," Taglioni laughed, "the tourists couldn't know of course, and the effect was just the same; but that bishop— he had just arrived, an American from Washington. You can't always tell, you see; but, as I said, it doesn't matter.

Yes, it's a strange thing, signori, the strangest thing about these mandarins. Every time I see them they take me back to Como, to that night, that Habañera, the twang of the guitar strings, the moonlight on the water—my little Neapolitan, with her red lips, her black eyes, her castanets clicking, her form like a Psyche. Alias— the Marchesa! Alias— one of the greatest lyric

The Bachelor Dinner

prima donnas on the Italian stage to-day!
Alias——"

Taglioni's eyes and Barry's met.

"Alias," he said slowly, "Mademoiselle Mimi!"

The Ghost of the Turret Chamber

A S Taglioni said this, the Doctor swung around in his chair suddenly and threw down his cigar, listening, half rising.

"What's the matter?" cried Travis.

"Didn't you hear something?" exclaimed Ménard. He looked up toward the gallery. "I thought—I was sure I heard some one calling."

We all shook our heads.

"Wait a moment! Wait a moment!"

He sprang to his feet, starting across the room toward the staircase; but quick as he was, Travis with a leap had reached it before him.

"Let me go, Doctor! Sit down, finish your dinner. I'll go!"

"No, you won't," said Ménard grimly. "My orders are precise and they've got to be carried out. The whole success of the experiment depends upon it. As the old woman said to her waiting relatives just before the end, 'The watched pot never boils, my friends; and besides there's no legacy.' You go back to your place, my boy. This is my funeral."

165

The Bachelor Dinner

He had laid his hand on the younger man's shoulder, evidently expecting it to yield from his path, to recede before his pressure, friendly yet insistent; but the expression of Travis' lower jaw I knew of old. It suggested, brought to memory, certain scenes on the gridiron; and the shoulder was a foot-ball one, used of old to resisting the onslaught of a team. The Doctor looked surprised. It was like running up against a rock at low tide where before was only water. The staircase was hopelessly, irremediably blocked.

"Why," he said—"sacrement! What a muscle you've got, man! Come, let me pass."

Travis smiled slightly. It was the smile we used to watch for, the smile that invariably preceded a tackle. It meant the ball was his, his opponent on the ground; it also meant a broken head generally for somebody, and a mounting of the score. Instinctively, from sheer force of association, I held my breath and waited. Travis' eyes were passionate but steady; they met the Doctor's keen ones. He seemed to be holding down, restraining some emotion.

"Nobody called you, Jacques," he said; "there wasn't a sound. You only imagined it. I'm going up myself to see. If she did, I'll let you know." He shook the hand from his shoulder and took a step forward; but Ménard, recovering himself, caught hold of him again by the sleeve, by the elbow.

"No, Travis! No, don't! What's the use, old man, of breaking up the company, deserting all your guests? Come back here; come back, I say! It isn't time yet. No. Just as you say, I must have imagined it. . . . You heard nothing, gentlemen?"

Still clutching Travis, he turned back to us eagerly as if seeking confirmation—help and backing in some crisis through which those two were passing, unknown, unshared, unsuspected by the rest.

"You heard nothing, gentlemen?"

At that moment Jean entered the room with the coffee.

"Ha," cried Nicot, "that was it! It was Jean outside swearing at the coffee grounds. Turkish coffee, oh, mon Dieu! Come back here, both of you. Mr. Whittemore tells me he has a story up his sleeve. That's the proper expression, eh? A ghost story—what? The real thing, too; just goes with Turkish coffee. Come along, Travis!"

"Come ahead, Doctor!"

The last was Barry's voice. To my astonishment the tone was strained, excited; almost—it was absurd—as if he too were pleading. They

167

The Bachelor Dinner

both seemed dead in earnest, to have set their hearts on something.

Travis half turned, and put his back against the rail. "Bring the coffee over here, Jean, to the window. Draw up the curtains, yes. Blow out some of those candles over there; lay the cigars on the stand. I'll be down again directly." With that he smiled again and shot up the staircase. At the top he waved his hand. "Make yourselves at home, gentlemen!" Then he pushed the door open and disappeared behind it.

"*Diable!*" said Ménard under his breath. He seemed worried, irritated, looked over at Nicot, and the two exchanged glances; but no move was made to follow.

As the valet went about silently, swiftly, carrying out his master's orders, we left the table, all of us, and moved toward the window. Through it was wafted a delicious, cool fragrance. The breeze caught the yellow curtains, blowing them a little. As the lower candles were extinguished the room was left in shadow. Each man sought an easy-chair. The cigars, pipes and cigarettes were relighted. Whether it was physical comfort or mental uneasiness, the after effect of the dinner or the twilight, heaven only knows, but no one said a word.

Ménard's eyes were fixed on the gallery. We all

followed his gaze instinctively. A feeling of restlessness, *malaise*, or was it premonition, crept insidiously, like a chill through the atmosphere. What was that event we were all waiting for?

Presently the door flung back and Travis reappeared. His face looked flushed in the candlelight, his voice had the ring of excitement in it. He hurried straight down the staircase toward Ménard. "How is that?" he cried out. "How is that? . . . She isn't there!"

"Not there?" exclaimed Ménard. He made a sudden move as if to spring to his feet; then controlled himself with an effort, speaking hurriedly. "The flame's burning, is it?"

"Yes, the flame's burning."

"Any change since you saw it?"

"Oh slight, slight; nothing to speak of. Still a dead white."

"No color at all?"

"No color at all. . . . Ménard, that's queer!"

"What? No, I don't think so; it's too soon." The Doctor raised his coffee-cup to his lips quietly, tasting the contents, scenting the aroma. "Excellent this, Travis—couldn't be better; has the real Eastern flavor. The last time I drank it was in Constanti——"

"The woman— the woman, I mean!" broke in

169

The Bachelor Dinner

Travis. "She's gone, don't I tell you? The flame is burning alone! She isn't there!"

Again came that half movement, suppressed, like a twitching of the muscles, an involuntary starting up; then the Doctor relaxed. The coffee-cup was still at his lips; and he emptied it slowly before he answered, draining it to the dregs. "That's all right, Travis; that's all right. She's had her instructions. I know that woman and I've tested her; she'll follow them. When the thing's ready, when the proper time comes— By the way, Mr. Whittemore"— he turned to Barry brusquely, almost roughly, as if to break off the conversation — "what was that story you were just about to tell us? The ghost story— eh? Now we're sitting here in this spooky half-light, it's just the right moment. Have you got another bogie, sir, to match that tale of mine?"

Barry laughed and glanced at Travis.

"Here, sit down, old man; here's your coffee! Want a match? . . . Yes, a few years ago I had an experience, a real, genuine, face-to-face encounter. You don't believe in ghosts, Doctor; and none of the rest of you do, I dare say. Well, I didn't either. That's the sort of thing you have to go through once yourself. After that— br-r-r!" He drew in his shoulders. "The very remembrance of that dark night makes me shiver! Talking of

The Ghost of the Turret Chamber

Como, gentlemen," he nodded to Taglioni, "it was just there, strangely enough—I couldn't help recalling it while monsieur told his story—just exactly there it happened. And I've never mentioned it to a single living soul, not even to McD. here. What's the use? You won't believe it."

Taglioni made a swift sign with his forefingers crossed and glanced about the studio. "*Già, già!*" he said, whispering. "In those old Italian villas, where the walls are mouldering and the loggias overhang the lake, and those huge salles are empty more than half the year round—*tante strane cose* happen! Any caretaker could tell you. It's best to make the cross always to avoid the evil eye. Where you find a beautiful villa deserted, the garden running riot, cobwebs over everything and bats in the eaves, only an old cicerone on the ground, the strangers, when he shows them about, wonder; but that's generally the reason. All Italians know it. Was that your case, signore? Did you visit one after the Ave Maria, after nightfall?"

"No," said Barry, "not exactly. The widow of a friend of mine, a client, was living there. An Italian lady, belonging to one of the old Lombard families who had lived in that same villa for several generations. Her husband, a handsome fellow, had died rather suddenly. They had investments in America; and my going there was purely on a matter of business. I was passing through Milan, and I went down to see her. It was June, I remember; the season far advanced, the flowers all in bloom. So hot that we were sitting on the terrace all the evening. You have seen the place, of course, sir?"

He looked over toward Taglioni.

"An old villa, surrounded by cliffs, set back; the terrace high and spacious, shaded with magnolias; a narrow, moss-grown staircase winding downward to the lake. Just a rambling pile of stucco, built in several layers of different stories each; rose-colored to start with, but rain-washed, weather-beaten. The turrets smothered with ivy; the garden dense with palm-trees, rhododendron, cactus; and a huge old cedar that spread its branches over all, darkening the doorway.

Because of the cliffs, the wildness of the coast there, no other villa, no neighbors existed, not for miles either side. A goat path led back across the cliffs to a straggling village several kilometres distant and a little old pilgrimage church, from whose yellow campanile you could hear the bells at sunset. Except for this, the only entrance, the only exit to the villa was by boat. The landing

The Ghost of the Turret Chamber

hemmed with rocks; and then that steep, dark staircase. The porto guarded by a satyr, motionless, hoofed and horned, moss-covered, ancient.

In this spot," said Barry, "beautiful, I grant you, but lonely and uncanny—the Contessa, since the death of her husband, lived alone, absolutely alone with a pair of old servants. Not a friend, not a neighbor, not a diversion; not a living soul of her own class to speak to. The padre from the village came to dinner once a week; said mass in the chapel, heard the confessions and gave absolution. That was all.

On the night that I speak of, this same padre— Don Leone they called him—had been invited down to the villa to meet me; and the three of us were sitting all together on the terrace, watching the starlight, talking a little, scenting the magnolias.

The Contessa was young still, a strange-looking woman—black hair, great black bruises under her eyes, a face like alabaster; the expression of some one habitually nervous, almost unhinged, who has had some great shock. At least so I read her. But of course ill health, sorrow, the lonely, abnormal life she was leading, even the shadow cast by the cedar under which her low chair stood, were enough to account for almost anything, I thought. She was rather silent; but something

The Bachelor Dinner

about her, a certain charm, illusiveness, I don't know what, appealed to me.

The night, in spite of the stars, was a dark one. The rough water tossed and surged against the balustrade below. A mass of clouds, heavy, threatening, sinister, covered the mountain passes that lead over into Switzerland. The heat was still oppressive. Here and there, afar off, came the rumbling of thunder; and across the lake, suddenly, fitfully, now one side, now the other, lightning flashed and disappeared.

'Odd thing, that!' I said. 'If it weren't for the storm coming— By Jove, Contessa, am I wrong or not? Isn't that a search-light?'

She gave a quick look up and nodded.

'That's a curious business! I've been watching that light now ever since it first started, wondering about it. First it races up and down the coast; then it plunges head first to the base of those mountains; then it leaps straight out to the centre of the lake, and dashes up and down there. Pretty agile lightning, that! Almost looks— ha! Any motive there, padre; anything behind it?'

'Oh, no,' he said, 'no!' The old man drew his soutane closer. A light breeze had sprung up. 'Will you have your shawl, Contessa? . . . *Dio mio!* Everyone on Como knows that, signore. When the flash-light plays they are looking for smugglers.'

The Ghost of the Turret Chamber

'Smugglers?' I exclaimed.   'What!... Where do they come from?'

'Over the mountains, signore, from Lugano. Behind those dark patches where the light is searching now, there are trails down the gorges. On the lake somewhere their boats lie hidden, waiting, without any light astern, the oars silent, muffled.   But no one ever sees them.'

'Any caught lately?'

The old priest shook his head.

'Ha!' I cried, 'you mean to say— That's odd! They never catch them?'

'Eh, signore? *Mai!* Not in my lifetime. Every night the light plays; flashes just so always, here, there—searching.   But it never finds, *mai!* Sometimes you hear gunshots; but they never reach the smugglers.'

'There must be a reason for that, padre.   How do you explain it?'   I turned to the Contessa.

She was leaning forward listlessly in her chair, staring blankly down at the water, half heeding. It was then for the first time that I noticed the bats. Gentlemen," said Barry, "under that cedar, darting in and out among the branches, swooping sometimes so low that they all but grazed her cheek—there must have been a dozen! Br-r-r!   The fell, black, menacing creatures!   I never saw so many together in my life."

175

The Bachelor Dinner

Both Barry and Taglioni shuddered simultaneously. Again the latter with a swift, secretive gesture moved his forefingers, crossed them like a flash. My friend took up his coffee-cup and sipped from it, musing.

"Very good, Travis, yes; the Doctor was right! Strangely enough it was Turkish coffee we were drinking that evening; and somehow, some way it got on my nerves. From the moment that I saw those bats— why I can't tell you, but the most extraordinary feeling came over me, a sort of dry shiver, premonition, almost fear. To shake it off, relieve it, I forced myself to speak, carelessly, naturally, pointing to the beasts.

'You are not nervous at all, Contessa? An American girl would dodge or run or cover up her hair. But perhaps here in Italy the claws are——'

Scarcely were the words framed when the Contessa gave a cry, a low sound, half articulate; gazing toward me, gazing past me, her form upright, trembling.

'I *pipistrelli! Madonna! I pipistrelli!*' she screamed. 'Drive them off, drive them away! How long have they been there? Ah, ah, *Dio mio!* Help me up, padre!'

With a second cry that chilled the blood she leaped out of her chair. Swathing her head in

176

The Ghost of the Turret Chamber

her lace mantilla, dodging, she sprang from under the cedar to the door and disappeared. The priest and I, left alone, turned and stared at one another. His face seemed blanched in the shadowy light— about as now, gentlemen, not a bit clearer. Well, you know what the effect is. For the matter of that you all look about the same. The Doctor there, and Travis— pale as ghosts!"

Barry stopped, caught himself up, and then went on hastily.

"Of course, as I say, it might have been the light; but the old chap had a worried look, and he watched me pretty keenly, stuffing the tobacco into his pipe-bowl, never opening his mouth. We both waited a moment, and then I took the lead.

'Sad, isn't it?' I said. 'Poor lady! Yes, it's just as I suspected. How long has she been that way?'

'Eh— what way?'

The priest dropped his pipe and stared.

'Why'—I touched my forehead—'so!'

By George, how that fellow jumped! 'Mad?' he cried, '*pazza?* Never! She's as sane, sir, as you are. *Santa Maria!* If you knew, if you guessed, what the poor soul has been through. Ah, these *pipistrelli!*' The old man clenched his teeth as a bat swooped past his shoulder, shaking his fist after it, muttering. '*Poverina, poverina!*

The Bachelor Dinner

You do not know perhaps, signore,'—he lowered
his voice and glanced hastily behind him, 'the
place is cursed—haunted!'

'Haunted?' I exclaimed.

'*Già!* It happened first long ago in the old
Principe's time. You see that turret yonder?'

It was behind me," said Barry, "where the
Contessa's eyes were riveted, rounding off the
balustrade, built of gray stone and set into
the stucco, apparently an afterthought though
shrouded thick with ivy—my gaze followed that
of the priest with curiosity. The turret was two-
storied, Gothic-pointed, slender, windowless except for slits, and these half covered over. At the
foot a door, also covered, partly hidden; all around
magnolias. And below, the rocky cliffs, falling
sheer, picturesque, precipitous, straight into the
lake.

Even as we gazed up, something small, black,
mouse-like, slipped noiselessly through one of the
apertures, swooping down, vanishing. The priest
made the sign of the cross, sinking back.

'*Vedi!*' he cried, '*vedi!* You see how it is? Not
a servant, not a *contadino*, not a soul in all this
region would dare to cross that threshold. Since
the night the thing happened, since the— *Madonna mia!*' He stopped short, mopping his
forehead with his handkerchief.

The Ghost of the Turret Chamber

'*Già, già!* It is true, signore, what I tell you. How it happened, or why, the devil only knows! They found the old Principe stiff and stark one morning, after a night spent up yonder, with an expression on his face indescribable! Br-r-r! As though he'd been together with Satan himself. The door was locked and double-locked. They had to burst it open. The windows— you can see for yourself, they are slits. The turret chamber was empty, deserted. Only the Principe —God rest his soul!—stretched out on the hearth- stone; and the *pipistrelli* swooping, with their nests among the eaves. Since then— it happened be- fore my day, signore, but I had it from the padre who was priest here in my place— the *contadini* avoid the turret, the terrace, even this portion of the lake after nightfall. They say— it is only a rumor, of course, and perhaps superstition——'

The old man glanced behind him, shrinking close to my shoulder, whispering. 'In the night the ghost walks. Sometimes, for a while, for even weeks together, there are no *pipistrelli*. Then all at once, presto! as to-night, they come in clouds. On those nights— it's just as sure, they say, as the way the wind blows and its bearing on the weather —things are heard, things are seen. It's best to stay indoors. Then, not for five hundred *lire*, signore, not for a thousand, would any *contadino*,

not even a regiment of strong men together and
backed up by muskets, pass the threshold of that
chamber. Of what use are bullets against the invisible! . . . *Dio*, did you feel that? Br-r-r!'

We both made violent, instinctive gestures to
drive the bats away; but as the night advanced—
whether it was the electric disturbance in the atmosphere, a presage of the coming storm, or a reason more uncanny, some hidden occult influence
to which they were sensitive— I'm sure I don't
know, gentlemen, but I never saw bats behave like
that before!"

Barry leaned forward suddenly, glancing about
him.

"Indeed it was those bats that really made me
first— By the way, McD., you remember, don't
you, how keen we both of us used to be about
that ghost society,"—he turned to me sharply,
"the one they had at Cambridge, of which our
own society was a branch? I was in it neck and
crop, searching out data, hunting down spirits. So
you can imagine, all this talk was so much game
for me. Still, by nature I'm a sceptic, and past
experience had taught me. The mere matter of
a scheduled ghost was no longer enough in itself
to make me turn a hair. Ninety-nine chances
to a hundred there was none. A murdered man,
a mouldy room, a locked door, a few hysterical

The Ghost of the Turret Chamber

subjects, suggestion for the rest; and there you had the whole matter in a nut-shell."

Barry stopped for a moment, knocked the ashes from his pipe and refilled it. "Match, Travis! Thanks."

During that moment there was silence in the studio. Then my friend resumed with the stem between his lips, his voice sounding strange, far away between the puffs.

"Yes, gentlemen— ninety-nine chances out of a hundred, yet the hundredth chance is there. It is that one possibility that makes the ghost societies, keeps the zest alive and fills out the reports. The instinct of the chase! I started in, like a reporter, to ply the priest with questions.

'Was nothing done, padre, nothing discovered? How was that? No sign, no clew? Did they search?'

'Oh, they searched,' he said, 'yes! The police came up from Milan. They tapped the stones and the walls, but by daylight of course. Is the law any use when it comes to evil spirits? If it were myself who owned the villa, signore, I should tear the turret to pieces with my own hands, stone by stone; and sprinkle each one with holy water until they glistened and shone like the rocks by the lake-side.' He gave a little shudder. '*Già!*'

The Bachelor Dinner

'You've seen the ghost yourself, then?'

He shrank back at once protesting. 'I, signore?
With the eyes— no! When the *pipistrelli* come
—you understand? One sees with the——'

'With the back of the neck, with the small of
the spine! A weird feeling, that! Yes,' said I,
'I felt the same, but it may have been the damp.
Has the Contessa ever seen it? With the eyes,
I mean.'

Don Leone's gaze was fixed, following the search-
light absently, steadily, as if he had not heard.

'Tell me,' said I, 'why does she have that scared
look in them; like a hare when the panting of
the hounds is at her heels? The Principe was her
father. Was it that? You must know.'

'Perhaps,' he said, '*chi lo sa!* Or it may have
been the——'

All at once, even as he spoke, his face changed.
Gentlemen," cried Barry, "his face went gray and
mottled like the bark of a eucalyptus! The
strangest effect of embarrassment, or terror, or
moonlight, I could not tell which. He turned
and caught my hand.

'But you heard, of course, signore? She told
you— the Contessa? Surely she told you how and
where the young Count died?'

'No,' I exclaimed, 'no, she didn't! It happened
in the autumn, if I remember rightly. Last

The Ghost of the Turret Chamber

September, wasn't it? He died— certainly they
wrote, or gave me that impression— the Count
died of fever.'

'Fever!' cried the padre. 'Sh-h-h!... Signore,
come closer, put your head lower, nearer mine
— so! Why, I supposed you knew. It's common talk up there in the village and all along
the lake-side. Those things get out somehow. I
would not have spoken, I would not breathe it
now, only— Sh-h-h!'

The old man was stooping, and his fingers
twitched in mine.

'Sh-h-h!... They found him dead. They
found him dead up there in the turret chamber!'
He pointed to it, staring, his voice shrunk to a
whisper. 'Up there, stretched out, just as the
Principe! The same expression on his face, the
door locked and double-locked, the room dark,
empty, the *pipistrelli* flying! He was there alone.
Why——'

'Why?' I cried.

'The devil only knows! It may have been the
sight of the ghost that killed him, that made his
heart stop beating. That is what they say, signore. It is always death for somebody when the
bats circle low. Just so it was before with the
Principe, with the Count— and now, to-night,
again. *Dio mio! Dio mio!* Do you wonder,

183

signore, that the poor Contessa fled? Since that night, since last September, they have never swooped like this.'

'It's the storm,' I said, 'padre!'

'No, signore, the ghost walks—the ghost walks! Poor lady! The place is like a hermitage; the flowers run riot with no hand to restrain them ever since the Count's death. *Davvero*, except for yourself, not a soul has come here! Look at the search-light on the water and smell the magnolias. Poor Contessa! She gives, gives with both hands. A saint, signore, an angel— and lives here alone like a nun in a cloister! Br-r-r! these *pipistrelli!*'

He rose slowly, drawing his soutane around him. 'It is growing chill and late. You will pardon me now if I leave you and retire? The path over the cliffs is narrow and steep. My rest is at the top; and soon the bells will be ringing for matins! *Buona sera*, signore.'

'*Buona notte*, padre.'

With that the old priest nodded, waving his hand, and turned up the path. In another moment he was gone, he had vanished in the darkness. I was alone," said Barry.

My friend took a long puff, shifted his pipe from one corner of his mouth to the other, puffed again, and then went on.

The Ghost of the Turret Chamber

"Now the thing I am going to tell you, gentlemen—as I said before, it's my own experience,
and you're welcome to hoot at me as much as
you please. This is what happened. It's a fact,
incredible, preposterous, as the truth often is.
Explain it if you can. I'm not nervous, I'm
not a drinking man, I'm not a fool; and there's
never been any insanity in the family. You see
this scar here?"

Barry's hair was light, curly, very thick. He
lifted a lock that fell over on his forehead, snatch-
ing up the nearest candle.

"You see this, gentlemen?"

Under the hair, hidden, was a deep indentation,
ugly, discolored. It looked like a bruise on the
bone that had not healed. The Doctor leaned
toward him quickly, half carelessly, and touched
it with his finger.

"A nasty blow—that! Had it some little time,
haven't you, Mr. Whittemore? Let me see!
Unconscious after it, of course, dazed, lost your
memory for a while—must have laid you out
quite flat!" Ménard spoke without the question-
mark. Evidently to him, the color, the position,
the handling told volumes.

Barry gave a grim laugh. "No optical illusion
about that, Doctor, is there? A man couldn't
very well dream a bruise, could he; or inflict it on

185

himself? I wanted you to look at it before I told the story. Gentlemen, that night on Como I nearly met my death!"

The Doctor nodded assent gravely, still studying the scar. Taglioni looked up, startled. The rest of us, moving as if with common impulse, drew the circle closer. For a moment even the smoking was suspended. We leaned forward listening.

"Eh? . . . Diable!" cried Nicot.

I sat and stared at Barry. "What in the name of——"

"That's all right, McD.," he said; "that's all right. Have a cigarette? . . . As a matter of fact I never told you at the time, and I never made any report to the society. There were reasons enough; you will all understand this. As long as the Contessa still lived it was impossible. But now, now," Barry stopped and glanced about him, "the seal is off my lips. After the padre left me that night—it must have been half an hour or so, perhaps longer—I was still smoking, dreaming under the cedar, the bats still circling, when suddenly the storm broke.

All through the evening the clouds had been gathering, the thunder rumbling, the atmosphere heavy, oppressive, lifeless. When the rain finally fell, it was after a thunder-clap so terrific, so explosive, it was like the last judgment! The light-

The Ghost of the Turret Chamber

ning seemed to rend the clouds, a jagged streak across the sky, blood-red as if the heart of the world had been knifed. A few drops here and there, scattered, and then it came in sheets. Within a second everything was swallowed up in blackness. Before I could spring to my feet," said Barry, "before I realized what had happened or could even make a movement, the terrace, myself, the whole place was deluged. Instinctively running, groping, with my arms over my head, I leaped for the nearest door; rattled at the lock, which stuck—Italian locks always do— pressed it back and dashed inside.

Jove!" said Barry, "my clothes were drenched through! What with the violence of it, the sudden onslaught, I never met anything like it before. Those tropical storms, to me, always have something supernatural, demon-like about them. Whether it was that or the chill, I don't know, but my spine began to creep, my very teeth to chatter. It was then, and not till then, that I noticed where I was.

Instead of the side entrance, the one I thought I made for—the door, small, rusty, evidently unused, opened into the turret. Beyond wound a staircase. Only the first dozen steps were visible, beyond that darkness. Above, ahead, the bats alone made the location unmistakable— be-

The Bachelor Dinner

yond was the turret chamber. In that moment, gentlemen, even as I stood there with the door half open, the rain driving in, peering in front of me shivering, undecided, a clock far off in the distance began to strike, rhythmically, the tone resonant. It chimed twelve strokes. Should I go on, should I turn back, should I stay where I was? The rain and the ghost society decided me.

Now as you know,"—said Barry, "a burnt child dreads the fire, but up to then I'd not been burnt. Deliberately, of course, one would never venture to spy without permission on anybody's premises, least of all on your hostess, or even on a ghost; but circumstances, as you can see for yourselves, forced me. I had watched for ghosts before, but always in vain. Did they exist or not? If so, why were they there?

The question, always open, never solved, tempted me. This was my opportunity. Alone, unhampered, with all the night before me, clear-headed, empty-handed, full of curiosity, the investigator's instinct drew me on," said Barry. "Stepping lightly, moving cautiously, the darkness seemed to close around, falling like a curtain. Except for the whir of the bats as they brushed me, an occasional glimmer through the slits of the wall, the patter of the rain outside, the place was like a tomb. Gentlemen——"

The Ghost of the Turret Chamber

Barry stopped and gave an odd laugh. "Those spiral stairs seemed endless. I felt each step with my foot before I climbed it, clutching the circular wall with one hand, while the other groped the darkness. If you've ever watched a caterpillar pushing blindly with his feelers out—that was my case exactly. All at once—how it came or why I can't explain—I was conscious of a sixth sense: a sort of sight or consciousness dependent not on the eyes but on the nerves; not on the hearing at all, for there was nothing, but on those same abnormal, mysteriously developed feelers. Involuntarily, as from a blow, my whole body recoiled. There was something, someone near me.

What it was I couldn't tell; but a cold, clammy shiver seemed to seize me all over. My tongue clove to the roof of my mouth; my feet were numb, rooted. Not for the life of me," said Barry, "not to save myself from hanging, could I have spoken or stirred. When the sensation passed— it was almost like a trance—the blackness in front of me seemed to spread suddenly, losing itself beyond in a general mist, a vagueness, full of shadows, reflections. It was like gazing into a pool, empty, silent, not a ripple on the surface. Below the pool was movement.

Even as I gazed, slowly, gradually, the shadows took shape. Two of them were crouching di-

The Bachelor Dinner

rectly in front of me. My foot was on the last stair. The space, octagonal, vaulted, was that of the turret chamber. What it was they crouched beside, whether a coffin, a chest, or a hole, I could not tell; but out of it came vapor. The vapor curled, twisted like a snake, writhing upward. Now what followed, gentlemen— put it down to delirium tremens, if you like. As I watched, all at once, the impression was just as if a face floated toward me. I started back in horror. The face was that of a death-mask! As it approached, swift, silent, menacing, the blood stood still in my veins. I gave a cry.

'My God! . . . It's Agramonte!'

Before me rose the ghost of my dead client!

Barely had the name crossed my lips when something struck me. Whether by superhuman agency or not, whether it was merely the shock that felled me, I don't know, I shall never know!" said Barry, "but these were my sensations exactly in their sequence. A sudden rush of night air, something damp against my forehead, a whiz as of a bat's wing—and then my senses left me. Match again, Travis! . . . Thanks."

My friend's pipe, during the last minute or so, had gone out. He stopped and relighted it, stooping forward, shielding the bowl between his hands. Ménard glanced at the scar and nodded.

The Ghost of the Turret Chamber

"When I came to," said Barry slowly, "I was lying on the bed in the guest room of the villa, with a nursing Sister in charge. It was several days later. She said, I'd had a fall that night on the terrace, they had found me under the cliff; ever since then I had lain unconscious. That was all she seemed to know. The Contessa herself was ill. As soon as I could move, I left. I never saw her again. . . . That's a pretty bit of coloring on your meerschaum, Travis. Took you long, did it? . . . Yes, gentlemen, that experience with the occult nearly cost me my life. I never want another. Since then I believe in spirits, have to— there's no other explanation. But," Barry lowered his voice, "I avoid them like the devil! What do you make out of it?"

The question was asked off-hand, in a general sort of way, and for a little no one answered. Then Taglioni, whose fingers were still crossed, spoke carelessly.

"You knew young Agramonte well, signore?"

"Oh, fairly, in a business way. We had met several times. Our firm had charge of his American interests."

"Rich, was he?"

"Rich for Italy."

"Did you ever meet his brother?"

"No."

The Bachelor Dinner

"Looked just like him, like as two peas! Handsome, dashing, North Italian type. *Già!*" said Taglioni.

He held his cigarette up and regarded it thoughtfully, his head against the carving of his chair, leaning back. We all went on smoking.

"*Sì*, signore— what you said about that searchlight. How I used to watch it! Every evening for years, ever since I can remember, it darts, flashes here, there, searching for those smugglers; all along that end of Como, to guard the mountain passes. Strange, they never find them!" he laughed.

"Well, it struck me so," said Barry. "When the padre told me, I couldn't help suspecting——"

"Suspecting what, signore?"

"That the smugglers had some strong influence, some power behind them, for one reason or another, that acted as a shield between them and the police."

"They have," said Taglioni.

As he spoke he twirled the cigarette around, still thoughtful, still examining it. "You know, sir, what the peasants say?"

Barry gave a start.

"The peasants there on Como—*sì*. The rumor is well known that an old Italian family, one of the oldest Lombard families, have made their

192

The Ghost of the Turret Chamber

fortune through it. On the lake, in some villa, the smugglers have their rendezvous. Who it is, of course, and where—" Taglioni lifted his shoulders. "But the head of the family and the chief of the smugglers is the same man, they say. You spoke of the Principe, of the Count, signore, It may be—*chi lo sa*—they died of some stray bullet. Both found in the turret chamber, brought there secretly, by stealth, perhaps by some mysterious, unseen entrance!"

"Jove!" cried Barry. "I believe you're right. And that is why the bats flew! Whenever their sanctum sanctorum was invaded, out they came, mad as hornets. You think it was the brother then—" he put his hand to his scar. "Is that the explanation?"

"Sh-h-h! . . . Sh-h-h, signore! Perhaps it is, perhaps it isn't! As long as Agramonte lives, and the search-light still plays, it is better not to say things. The smugglers have a long arm and, as you've proved, that arm can strike. You had a narrow escape, sir!"

Barry yawned, blew a whiff out of his pipe, and looked at Travis.

"Asleep, Dannie—eh? Wake up, old man!"

"What's that? . . . What's the matter?"

Travis started from his revery. His eyes were heavy, bloodshot, as one who has roused himself

The Bachelor Dinner

with an effort, whose mind has been absorbed.
Apparently Taglioni's last sentence was all he
had heard.

"Was that you speaking, Barry? Telling about
that old scar of yours, weren't you? Yes. How
long ago those football days seem, don't they?
You were telling about that scrimmage?"

Barry gave an odd laugh.

"Not exactly," he said, "no. What a memory
you've got, man! Nothing half so important! . . .
Want to fill your pipe, old chap?" He leaned
forward suddenly and laid his hand on Travis'
shoulder.

"It was just a little tale about a Ghost—and a
Turret Chamber."

The Pound of Flesh

"OH," said Travis, "I thought— or was it the other side?"

He gave a queer glance at Barry, half keen, half indifferent; then his brooding eyes fastened themselves on the Doctor.

"What time are you, Ménard?"

As he said this he took out his own watch, consulting it. The surgeon never budged.

"What time did you— did you say she was coming, Doctor?"

Ménard puffed out a cloud of smoke and looked up. Barry was busy pulling at his lock, arranging it over the scar on his forehead; he seemed amused at something. The gaze of the two men crossed for a second; then Ménard turned to Travis.

"Why? What's your hurry, Dan? . . . If you'd spent a long day in the laboratory as I have, you'd want to smoke in peace. The thing can't come to a head possibly for another half hour, probably longer; and besides, the woman's there. She's watching, she'll report. The moment that the——"

The Bachelor Dinner

"But she isn't there!" cried Travis. "Didn't I tell you!"

"Oh, yes, she is, Dannie."

"Well, she wasn't a few minutes ago," said Travis irritably. "I searched the whole place over. Suppose I——"

"No, no!" The Doctor threw down his cigar rather hurriedly and half rose, resting his hand on Travis' arm. The touch was like a steel clamp, riveting him to his seat; but the tones of his voice were soothing. "No, Dannie, no, old man; sit quiet, can't you? It won't be much longer now. I've left that little woman in charge of the test-tubes. She knows what she's about, and I've every confidence in her—every confidence." He raised his voice slightly.

"A woman of that type, that particular type—If you had studied women as I have, Travis, you wouldn't have been deceived. Why, for faithfulness, devotion—she'd stick to her post up there if the whole place exploded! And if she promised to do a thing, she'd carry it out to the letter; to the letter, my boy, no matter if it killed her." Ménard's voice rang out. He leaned over, still standing, pressing down on Travis' shoulder. His face was grim, expressionless; he went on speaking rapidly. "The only weakness in a woman of that sort—it's a well-known fact to any student

196

The Pound of Flesh

of psychic law—is a mania for self-sacrifice, to-ward the whole world if necessary, but especially toward those they love—toward those they love, gentlemen."

He bit his lip, hesitated, then rapped the words out sharply.

"If that woman up there—you can take this for a case in point—if she dreamed for an instant, if she got it into her head that there was danger in our little experiment upstairs, an explosion, say, imminent, and she heard a foot on the stair, she'd be capable, perfectly capable, of bringing it on ahead; letting herself be blown to atoms to save the—the man she——"

The Doctor steadied himself.

We all sat there startled. The sudden tense-ness in his voice, the feeling in his manner, left little room for doubt. What was driving him to it? What hidden force impelled him? A man of strong reserve in the midst of comparative strangers! Was he drawing the veil from his own life's secret? Every man sat motionless. Ménard, after a moment or two, continued. He had thrown himself back in his arm-chair by this time, and had turned away from Travis, his eyes fixed strangely, tenderly on that little door in the gallery.

"In such a case," he went on slowly, "ninety-nine women out of a hundred would scream, rush down the stairs, hide behind the man—think of themselves first. The hundredth would do as I've just told you. It's madness, of course. Most men, particularly the virile kind, prefer the others. Still, it's the finest type of woman; it's the kind that makes for heroes in another generation."

Ménard took up his cigar, relit it. In the half-light, the grimness of his face was touched with shadow, the muscles seemed to soften. Almost, I could have sworn, his lips were pressed together, his strong mouth was quivering. Travis moved uneasily. He seemed about to ask a question when Nicot interrupted.

"Ninety-nine out of a hundred, Doctor! Nine-hundred and ninety-nine out of a thousand you mean. From my experience of women they're not much to rely on, charming, alluring, indispensable as they are. You're lucky if you've found the exception!" He laughed.

The laugh seemed to jar on Ménard. He turned his back roughly and began to talk to Barry. Nicot puffed his cigarette.

"Talking of exceptions, by the way, Doctor, there's another type of woman you haven't even mentioned, as far removed from the type up there"—he waved his hand toward the gallery and laughed again shortly—"as the two poles, gentle-

The Pound of Flesh

men, as the earth from the sky, as heaven from hell! And yet——" he glanced over at Ménard, "What you said was true, Doctor. It's the women who cower behind them, men understand the best. But the kind that drives them stark mad, that makes their pulse beat faster and sends the blood to their brains, that's another sort still. Luckily for the world an exception, like the other. Have you ever met it, Doctor?"

The surgeon shrugged his shoulders.

"The woman I mean," said Nicot, "would send a man to his death, would save her own little finger at the expense of the whole universe, would sacrifice her dearest friend for the sake of a moment's ambition. It's curious, unaccountable. No one has ever explained it, but wherever you find a woman, a woman like that, the men are at her feet. Whichever way she chooses to lead, they follow; whatever the rhythm of her pipe, they have to dance. You hear of such women, and read of them, Doctor, but in all your experience— I've often wanted to ask you the question." Nicot paused and knocked his ash off. He seemed confused for a moment. "Tell me honestly, Ménard, have you ever really met one?"

As the question was put in a low voice, with emphasis, we all stopped smoking suddenly, and a strange, electric silence laid its spell on our little circle. The pipes hung suspended, the smoke wreaths floated motionless. The gaze of every man there, roused to sudden interest, straining through the half-light, was focussed straight on the surgeon.

Ménard leaned his head back. With his eyes half closed, the smoke all about him, it was difficult to tell. Was he watching the gallery or not? Would he simply ignore the question, or was he debating his answer? The silence was a long one, but at last the Doctor broke it. He broke it with a drawl, his eyes still closed, puffing.

"The type, er—you mean, Nicot? . . . Yes, I met it once in Africa."

"Africa!" we all exclaimed.

Ménard settled back a little.

"You never ran across a mahogo-tree, gentlemen? A sort of sandal-wood! No? . . . Well, it's an odd sight, but not uncommon there. A fine, tall mahogo-tree, with a fig-vine twined about it. It grows up the mahogo very prettily at first, up and down the trunk, festooning the branches. Little by little the tendrils reach out, thicken. You can watch it, stage by stage. The vine becomes a tree. The more the fig-tree branches, waxing stronger day by day, the more the poor mahogo is smothered, overpowered. At last the

The Pound of Flesh

foliage of the fig completely hides the other; the mahogo-tree is dead. A skeleton, locked in the heart of its rival. While the fig itself, my friends—it's a fact, strange, unnatural, ghoulish as it seems. When the deadly struggle is over, there is no statelier, larger, more beautiful shade-tree in all that part of Africa, nor one more widely sought after.

I have sat under it often and pondered," said the Doctor, "why the parasite succeeds, why the egotist is loved. Oh, yes, there are such people." He spoke slowly, thoughtfully. "But really, Nicot, if you ask me, as far as I remember, I've met men like that, a few, but not—no never, I think, a woman. Not in real life. They may exist, they probably do, but outside of novels and newspapers I've never happened across them."

"Haven't you?" said Nicot. He twirled his cigarette loosely, staring down at the floor.

"No." The Doctor turned around. "Why, er—have you?" His tone was rather surprised.

Nicot flushed. "Yes," he said, "yes, I have; a woman just like that. Your story of the fig-tree fits her case exactly. She'd twine up a mahogo-tree, or anything or anybody that happened to take her fancy; and live on it and thrive on it, and grow more beautiful, more bewitching, more sought after each day, while her poor—"

The Bachelor Dinner

He stopped short. "I must say I pity that mahogo-tree, Doctor."

"So do I," said Ménard.

The rest of us all laughed, then waited expectantly. It was evidently some experience of his own that Nicot referred to; one that had touched him closely, that had left its mark deep. He still looked a trifle flushed; his half-cynical, half-careless ease of manner had vanished. Even his tongue failed him. He sat there as awkward, self-conscious as a school-boy.

"Go ahead!" said Ménard. "Go ahead! . . . What's the matter?"

Nicot remained silent, still twirling his cigarette.

"Let's hear about your fig-tree, Count. Who is she? Where did you meet her?"

By this time it was clear enough, Nicot repented having spoken and wanted to change the subject. The Doctor must have noticed this as well as the rest of us, but he went on inexorably.

"Yes, as I told you, Nicot, I've never run up against a woman of just that type; and really you interest me, interest me exceedingly. One of your youthful adventures, was it, or something more recent?"

He glanced at Nicot casually.

"Why," said Nicot, "rather recent. In fact—

202

The Pound of Flesh

Sacrebleu, Doctor!" Again he looked self-conscious. "You seem to have a sixth sense! The thing— a most extraordinary encounter it was too, only happened last week. I didn't mean to speak of it, but now—" he stammered, caught himself up, then continued hurriedly.

"The trouble is, this woman is so well known. You've all seen or heard of her, and the matter is rather delicate. No one dreams, at least so far as the world goes, that she has that side to her character."

"Of course not," said Ménard, nodding. "Of course not. The foliage of the fig is so green, so luxuriant, that the corpse inside is hidden."

"Exactly," cried Nicot, "and that's what makes it peculiar! I doubt if there is another man in Paris who knows the facts as I do; and I only found them out by the barest accident. A mere chance, gentlemen. You have all seen—" He stopped.

We all waited eagerly.

"Perhaps it's better not to mention names," said Nicot; "but if you guess, all right. The person I refer to, is one of the best-known actresses in France, and a very beautiful woman. You will find her face and figure photographed, painted, even on the post-cards, all along the Rue de Rivoli. Wherever she acts the theatres are crowded. The

The Bachelor Dinner

Parisians go mad over her. Behind the scenes it is the same. To begin with, her talent is something extraordinary; and that combined with grace, such as you wouldn't find again if you ransacked Paris over, charm, esprit, abandon, a personality that fairly carries you by storm—why, there's hardly an actress more popular, more surrounded!"

As Nicot paused for breath, the men around the circle began to smile, exchange glances.

"So you've guessed?"

Ménard laughed.

"Well, don't speak, don't say anything. Wait till you hear the story." Nicot put up a warning hand that held the circle in check, and then lowered his voice.

"It was last Sunday night, gentlemen. You remember what a balmy spring-like evening it was. I was dining out at the Pré Catelan about seven or thereabouts. The head-waiter there is a protégé of mine, in fact I got him his place; and he was helping me to pick out a choice little menu, with just the right vintage to give an epicurean flavor. Our heads were over the wine list, my shoulder half turned to the room, when suddenly a couple arrived at the table just opposite. The man nothing special, an insignificant, weak-kneed, caddish-looking chap; but the woman— as she swept by, every one turned and

The Pound of Flesh

looked at her. That little flutter, you know, when some one of prominence passes. A ripple over the atmosphere, a hush, and then a whisper. It was that that made me turn. Pierre looked up also. Meanwhile the couple were seating themselves, and I saw who the woman was.

We had met several times, here and there," said Nicot, "but she meets thousands of people, and I doubted if she knew me. At any rate no sign was made. Pierre had rushed to her side, evidently in a state of nervous exaltation to be waiting on such fame. My order was neglected. He bowed, scraped, suggested things humbly, cringing by her elbow. The great actress sat there, her lorgnettes raised, her manner haughty, tossing her orders to him over her shoulder. Her companion sat mum.

Whether there had been a quarrel or not," said Nicot, "it was difficult to tell, but the relations seemed rather strained between them. She was superbly gowned. A huge hat covered her ash-blond hair; her complexion was marvellous, delicate as satin. Her eyes were bright, sparkling, imperious. More beautiful, *au naturel*, than I had ever seen her, even on the stage, even made up. The entire room was magnetized; they couldn't take their eyes off. Unconcerned, nonchalant, she went on ordering, never glancing at the man, never addressing a syllable to him. He looked a whipped dog."

Nicot reached out for another cigarette and began again to play with it. There was still a touch of constraint, embarrassment in the Count's voice and manner, as if at some remembrance, disagreeable or otherwise, that he was loath to share. We all waited, smoking.

"Well," said Nicot, "the meal was just about half-way over. Up to that moment not a word had been exchanged, when all at once the actress leaned forward, said something. What it was I couldn't hear; but the man turned red as fire, leaped up, overturning the chair with a crash, and dashed out of the room. She threw back her head and laughed. A light, pearly titter, like a stage laugh, it was. We all sat dumbfounded. Before I could turn my eyes away—staring straight at her, the table with its vacant place, the overturned chair which the waiter was picking up, every soul in the restaurant craning over their shoulders—suddenly, to my horror, she turned around and beckoned. Smiling, with a gesture of intimacy, appeal, as if catching sight of an old friend opportunely, a friend who couldn't fail her, she beckoned to me," said Nicot.

"Gentlemen, imagine if you can what I felt! The blood ran cold in my veins. In the face of

The Pound of Flesh

the whole restaurant to snub such a woman as that
—the thing was simply impossible. One awful
moment passed, a moment that seemed hours.
Then I left my seat and joined her. Her hand-
shake, her greeting was cordiality itself; her
manner gracious, charming. With her hand still
clasping mine, she smiled up in my face.

'Stay with me, Count; do. Mon Dieu! Uncon-
genial company is worse than none, but a sympathetic companion is better than either. Have
your wine brought over!'

So Pierre rearranged the dishes, I sat down
vis-à-vis. For five minutes, gentlemen, through
the back of my head, I seemed to see that roomful,
every eye on us. Cold chills ran down my spine.
Suppose a friend should turn up, or any one who
knew me! The position was unpleasant. But
the five minutes passed. All at once the zest for
the adventure came over me. To be in the society
of the most beautiful, the most talked-of, the most
sought-after woman in all Paris, is after all something. Her voice was in my ear, her manner was
intoxicating—or it may have been the old vintage." Nicot laughed.

"At any rate, gentlemen, after that, a more
delightful hour I never spent with anybody. We
talked of art, letters, the stage, science, everything
imaginable. Soon the surroundings, the people

no longer existed. The time flew like magic. At last— just how the subject came up, I don't remember, but we mentioned the Russian dancers. She spoke of one particularly, with enthusiasm for her art, but slurring over her beauty. I differed with her, protesting.

'Chic,' she said, 'I grant you, *mais*—' The actress shrugged her shoulders.

'Blondes are more beautiful, of course,' I insisted—this to soothe her, gentlemen—'but for a brunette, the olive-skinned Slavic type, that little black-eyed dancer beats anything I ever saw! I doubt if there is a woman, a brunette, in all France who can hold a candle to her.'

We were arguing rather hotly, I more to tease her than anything else; but, like most beautiful women, she took the subject of beauty very seriously.

'You really think so, Count?'

'Of course I do, madame.'

To my surprise the actress sat perfectly still for a moment, staring down at her plate. 'You doubt if there is any one like her in Paris?' She repeated the words with a certain significance.

'I doubt it, madame, certainly.'

'Well, you're wrong then. There is one.'

I laughed rather mockingly.

'You don't believe me, Count?'

The Pound of Flesh

'Oh, sacré! . . . A woman's taste for another woman's beauty!'

'You won't take my word for it?'

'Seeing is believing, madame,' I said.

At that, all of a sudden she sprang to her feet. Her eyes had a curious expression in them, her soft chin was set.

'Very well!' she cried. 'Come with me, Count; now, this very moment! I'll introduce you to her! . . . Come!'

What made me hesitate and draw back, gentlemen, I really don't know; but she caught on instantly. Opposition, another will against their own, seems to madden some natures. The more I protested, the more determined she grew.

'Don't talk to me about that square-faced little Russian! If you want to see a real brunette, the most beautiful brunette in all Paris to-day! Don't you suppose I know what I'm talking about? Why, I know her well, intimately. My wrap, Count; here's the check. Your hat, your stick! . . . Come!'

All this time the actress was standing, both hands out, gesticulating, with the eyes of the whole room on her. Again a chill went down my spine, self-consciousness returned. Instinctively, hurriedly—it was useless to resist—I helped her on with her wrap, glanced once behind me, and fol-

The Bachelor Dinner

lowed her out of the restaurant. In a moment more, seated in her auto, leaning against the scented cushions with the famous actress beside me, we were whirling through the Bois.

The evening was delicious; the forest on either side stretched out mysterious. It was dark, lonely, late. After the first order, given in a low tone to the chauffeur at the start, not a word was spoken. The trees flashed by, the road stretched out ahead. Only gradually the notion dawned on me that we were racing away from Paris, away from the lights of the city as fast as the car could speed, into the open country.

'Ha!' I exclaimed. 'Diable!'

She had nestled back in the corner with her face half hidden, a scarf over her hair. The chauffeur's back was stolid. Evidently not a tone of my voice had reached them, it was lost in the rush of the car. Unless I pitched the chauffeur out and took the wheel myself, I was helpless in their hands. So I calmed down and waited. Gentlemen—" Again Nicot seemed embarrassed. He hesitated for a second or two, then went on.

"Half an hour exactly from the time we left that restaurant—I marked it by my watch—the auto drew up at a small villa. It was situated in the midst of a park, off the main road, with a fountain in front, surrounded by shade trees.

The Pound of Flesh

The loneliest, most forsaken little place you ever saw. As we entered the gate a hound began howling, taken up in chorus. In the gloom of the night the sounds seemed all around. The house was well guarded at least, that was evident. Then the auto stopped.

At the door, which was open, stood an old man," said Nicot, "a servant who met us. The hall inside was lighted. The servant led us in. No one seemed surprised, not the servant, not the actress. The latter lingered a moment behind and whispered. I stood like a dolt, staring about me, when all of a sudden a door beyond opened. It opened softly, noiselessly at my back, and a huge dog sprang out. The most splendid creature you can imagine," said Nicot, "a white Siberian wolfhound. He had his paws against my shoulder, and was licking at my face before I could wheel around—half fierce, half friendly, like an unrestrained puppy.

'Down, Loup! . . . Loup!'

At the sound of the voice the dog dashed back. I took a step forward. Before me was a square room, not large, low-raftered, the windows filled with flowers. Across one end stood a grand piano, and all around were books—an impression instantaneous of charm, of culture, which focussed like a flash on a figure in the centre.

The Bachelor Dinner

As I started back instinctively, I felt a hand on my arm.

'Count, allow me to present you to my sister,' said the actress."

"Ha, what— sister? Rubbish! Didn't know she had one!" Ménard gave a loud laugh. The rest of us exclaimed.

"Are you sure?" Taglioni interposed gently. "Why, that actress— she's well known among professionals. Her family are dead. But wait— no, you're right. I did hear something of an invalid sister several years ago. Just a mere rumor. You don't mean she's living still?"

"Living still!" cried Nicot. "Mon Dieu! The woman who was standing in the centre of that room didn't look much like an invalid. In all my experience of women—and I've met not a few of all countries and races—I never saw her match before. For sheer exquisite——"

Nicot's voice was husky suddenly. He stopped and cleared his throat.

"You may not believe me, gentlemen, but the first sight of that girl, that first distinct impression, has bitten into me like an acid. It is difficult to describe. She was standing with her hand on the wolfhound's collar, looking up timidly, a shy gaze like a child's. The eyes were like black stars. Her hair lay soft, shadowy about

212

her neck and brow, like moss on the bark of a silver-birch at midnight. Have you ever seen it growing? The bark itself gleaming white, translucent, satiny, with the moon-rays full upon it? Just so was her skin. Her form was slim, delicate. A young tree, too slender for the weight of the moss it seemed; and hidden here alone, unsought, in the very heart of the forest."

"The mahogo in the heart of the fig-tree— yes."

As Ménard interrupted, puffing a cloud of smoke, saying the words to himself half aloud in a dreamy voice, the Count went on without noticing.

"Not twenty miles from Paris, hardly out of sound of the great city's turmoil, yet the villa was like the grave. The room was so silent you could hear the crickets chirping, the sough of the wind outside, the hoot of an owl on the eaves. For a second," said Nicot, "after the introduction, after our gaze had met, I stood there transfixed. The actress broke the silence first.

'Eh, bien, Monsieur le Conte!' she exclaimed. 'Was I right or not? What did I tell you? . . . Hein?'

She moved forward gayly. In a moment more the three of us were seated together, talking like old friends. Again, as before, the hour simply flew. The conversation between us, flitting like a bird from topic to topic, brilliant, graceful, sympathetic, led as only Frenchwomen know how to lead. I shall never forget it, gentlemen. But the strange part, the unaccountable part, explain it as you may—little by little as the hour wore on, the personality of the actress, at first so strong, so dominant, faded and lessened before the force and charm of the other. That little star-eyed, slender girl, with all her shyness, inexperience, was like an electric flame by the side of a tallow candle. In the one you have the whole thing, at its best before you; in the other the power is turned on or off, mysterious, pervading. What causes it, what lies behind, its origin, development, capacity is hidden. But when the force is there—" he hesitated.

"You might as well blow out the candle," said Ménard.

"Exactly, Doctor. The personality of the actress, that night, was just like a candle with the extinguisher on it. Her talent seemed nil. Even her beauty, hot-house, artificial as it was, paled beside the brilliant coloring, the vitality of youth, the natural, untarnished genius of the other."

"Genius?" questioned Ménard. He voiced the thought of the circle.

"I say genius, gentlemen"—Nicot brought his hand down sharply—"yes, because it showed itself this way. Up to that moment the over-shadowing of the elder by the younger had been so subtle, neither woman seemed to realize it. Then, all of a sudden, we were talking of Racine, and a famous passage in *Phèdre* was under discussion. I had seen the play in Italy, and was arguing hotly for a certain interpretation. The actress felt it differently. The part was one she had often taken, one of her chief rôles; in fact the first that had made her famous. For all that the Italian, in that one passage, had understood it better, and I told her so frankly.

'What!' she cried. 'An Italian understand Racine better than a Frenchwoman? Mon Dieu—impossible!'

At that the sister leaped up. Her black eyes were blazing, her whole form was quivering. With her hands wrung together, leaning against the piano, she began to act the part—so suddenly, so fiercely, it was like one who had been struggling against some hidden fire and the flames had burst their bonds. Acting, gentlemen! It was more than that. She flung herself into that scene with a passion, an abandon I have never seen equalled. We sat there mute, gasping. The voice, the look was like a flail, lashing our emotions. From the first word to the last, convulsed, pleading, vibrant, Neither of us stirred.

The Bachelor Dinner

With the cry that ends it, a cry that not one actress in ten thousand dares to even attempt—the despair of it, the terror! To my dying day," said Nicot, "that cry will ring in my ears. The reality was something frightful; it made one's blood run cold. As the echo died away, the girl still standing there motionless, exhausted—suddenly, sharply, almost simultaneously the room door slammed, slammed to with fury! Gentlemen," said Nicot, "I started to my feet, turned; the actress wasn't there."

"Not there?" cried Ménard. "What!"

Nicot held up his hand to silence him.

"No," he said, "she was gone. And with the crash the girl turned white as chalk. She faltered, swayed. I sprang forward and caught her just in time."

"Where was the dog during this, Nicot?" Taglioni looked up suddenly.

"The dog was at her feet."

"Did he seem restless, alarmed, when she was acting—when she cried out?"

"Strangely enough, he didn't!"

"Not until——"

"Not until the door slammed."

"Must have been used to it then! I thought as much!" Taglioni exclaimed excitedly. "It takes years of practice to reach a point like that, even

The Pound of Flesh

with the greatest. But if she really had the training, as well as the genius that you insist on, Count,
then why in all God's earth—why has the world
never heard of her?"

"Why?" said Nicot. "Why? Ask the mahogo
why the fig-tree smothered it! . . . The scene in
that little room, gentlemen, that night, in the
dead silence and loneliness of the country, when
that poor girl poured her heart out— I shall never
forget it. We stood there together, the dog
crouched before us; she, clinging to my hand
like a child, trembling, her star eyes fixed on
mine. This is what she told me.

The youngest of a large family, all dead except
the actress, with fourteen years between them,
she had practically been brought up, looked after
by her sister, all her life as far back as she could
remember. Her talent showed itself early, and
was encouraged at first. She went through the
Conservatoire, graduated with a *premier prix*,
and began, as most of them do; a small part in
the provinces, with a travelling company. She was
just nineteen. After a little—I gathered this more
from what she didn't say than what she did—success began to come. With such talent as hers, such
beauty, it was bound to. The parts grew longer,
the local reviewers sat up suddenly and began to
take notice, the theatres lost their empty look.

The Bachelor Dinner

Then one day they made her understudy for the leading woman's part. The leading woman fell ill. That night her name was made.

A well-known manager happened to be in the audience and came to her behind the scenes. He offered her an engagement in Paris at the Odéon. She accepted, of course. Before the contract was signed, gentlemen— As the girl whispered it, her voice broken, stammering, she glanced over her shoulder, shivering all over. It wrung one's heart to see her.

'I sent a telegram to Thérèse,' she said. 'I thought she'd be so happy.' She wired back: 'Don't sign. Arrive in Lyons to-morrow night. Wait.'

At that time the actress' reputation was soaring up rapidly. She was playing in one of the best theatres in Paris, was photographed, run after. Her ash-blond hair, her dazzling skin, her sparkling eyes, her smile, they met you at every turn. A reputation that has gone on leaping forward in bounds from that moment to this. She was just past thirty-four, and the other was not yet twenty."

"*Dio mio!*" Taglioni started suddenly and gave an exclamation. "That's a queer thing, Count! What did the poor girl do?"

"Do!" exclaimed Nicot. "What could she do? She waited. The following night, very late, the

218

The Pound of Flesh

actress arrived, with her puppy dogs, her maid, her trunks, her automobile; and the two sisters met. The meeting took place in the actress' private room, with the shades drawn, the lights low, the door locked and double-locked. Until to-day not a soul in the world has ever dreamed what passed there."

Nicot stopped and wiped his brows.

"That poor child!" he said, "Remember, barely twenty; generous, tender-hearted, ignorant of her own powers, careless of her beauty—the actress for years like a mother to her, playing on her loyalty. Remember all this and condemn her if you can. The meeting was a tragedy. Imagine the two women, the one shaken, sobbing, the other down on her knees, imploring.

'Give it up for my sake! If you come out now, Baba' (that was her baby name) 'come out now, younger, more beautiful, while I am still on the boards! The Parisians are fickle. In a day you will be everything, I shall be nothing! Baba, if you love me! The life is nothing to you yet, you are young. You don't know what it is. To be thrown in the shade by you— I couldn't bear it! Swear to me you will do what I ask! As long as I live you will never appear! Swear to me, Baba! I will take care of you. You shall have a villa near Paris; horses, dogs, jewels, anything

you want! Only, don't show yourself unless
you want to kill me! I vow to you! I vow
to you!'

She pulled out a silver tube with some capsules
in it. 'That—unless you do!... Swear! Swear!
Swear!'

The girl sobbed, resisted, but the actress was
beside herself—a passion of terror, despair, emotion, that swept the child off her feet. Her
sister, remember, her own sister! The sight
of the poison did the rest! In the end she promised. Then she signed a paper. I saw it," said
Nicot, "a regular contract drawn up by an attorney, signed, sealed. She was never to act, never
to appear, never to obtrude herself in any way,
without special permission of the actress, during
the life-time of the same; and for that she received her living—nothing more, nothing less."

Nicot gave a grim laugh.

"Signed, sealed; yes, sir!... Gentlemen, that
contract reminded me of Shylock's. A pound of
flesh, to be delivered at such a date and day!
There was no Portia to help her. The pound of
flesh was delivered. Only worse, much worse!"

The Count's voice rose suddenly. His fist
crashed down on the table.

"For five years, gentlemen, five long years, that
young creature has lived in that villa buried, her

The Pound of Flesh

beauty never seen, her talent choking within her. Dogs, horses, books, her piano, an old couple to take care of her, the sight of the actress occasionally— that was all. And all that time the genius within her, growing, pulsing, drove her back to the dramas, the great parts she was made for. She studied them, acted them out, with the wolf-hound for an audience.

'You don't know what it is,' she cried; 'that impulse, that craving like a hunger inside of you, and not to be able to feed it!'

This with a shudder," said Nicot, "a frightened glance at the door! . . . My God, it must have been hell!"

For a moment or two there was silence around the circle; everyone pondered—a silence that was broken finally by Barry. He sat up, straightened, his lawyer's instinct pointing like a retriever after game.

"By Jove, that's a terrible story, Count! Incredible! You are sure the contract bound her?"

"Sure," said Nicot; "there wasn't a loophole."

"But suppose she paid the damages?" Barry insisted. "Actresses have often done it before."

"Not in this case."

"Why?"

"She has no money, except what her sister gives her."

The Bachelor Dinner

"Not a cent?"

"Not a *centime*."

"That's bad!" Barry shook his head and gave a long whistle. "Fettered for life then, tied up, handcuffed like a prisoner! Poor child! I should like to see the attorney who drew up such a paper."

"So should I!" said Nicot.

He moved restlessly, muttering the words through his teeth. The feeling in his manner was significant, unmistakable. Ménard, who was sitting with his eyes closed, smoking, opened one half way, gave a careless glance at the Count, swept it over the room, then closed it again. In the sweep he took in Travis. Dan was sitting listlessly, staring up at the gallery. His mind, rebellious while his body yielded, intent, absorbed, aloof, was searching the space beyond. As the Doctor saw this, a gleam flashed out suddenly; then the lid of the eye covered it.

"Very sad, Nicot," he said, "very tragic! I'm sorry for that young thing. There are only two ways out."

"What's that, Doctor?" Nicot spoke eagerly, turning from Barry. A flush had sprung to his cheek.

"Why send the attorney a challenge, shoot him, and then wait for the death of——"

"Yes, yes," cried Nicot, "I've thought of that;

The Pound of Flesh

but what good will it do? Meanwhile—it may be years you know—a smothered talent runs to seed, and the child is eating her heart out!"

"True," said Ménard. "Well, my friend, then there's only the other way left—to settle the case like Portia."

He began to declaim slowly:

'Tarry a little, there is something else.
This bond doth give thee here no jot of blood;
The words expressly are a pound of flesh.
Take then thy bond, take thou thy pound of flesh;
But, in the cutting it, if thou dost shed
One drop of Christian blood—'

"Stop!" cried Nicot. "What do you mean?" His face was pale, excited. He faced the Doctor, half rising.

"There is nothing in that contract against marriage surely?"

"No, no, of course not!"

"Then— if a man were rich, free, in love, it wouldn't be difficult to rescue her, would it? That is, in case she too——"

The Count started back. There was silence for a moment. Then without a word he leaned forward and gripped the Doctor's hand.

The Call of the Talent

A THRILL went over the atmosphere as Nicot did this, as he turned his face away, vibrating on our nerves like an electric current. No one spoke for a little; all thought the same thing. Why was Travis still watching the gallery?

Except for a start and a glance at Nicot just before the end, an impatient, rather bewildered look as if conscious of the thrill, resentful of that outside, mysterious something breaking into his thoughts, it was evident he had heard nothing. The creak of that door as it swayed in the breeze was like a magnet drawing him. Why did it draw him? What force lay behind it? Why had he left it open? The thought, subtle at first, subconscious, passed from mind to mind.

Nicot, his head bent, his back to the circle, stared down into the garden. DeJong and the General were both frankly interested, not in the Count, but in Travis. Taglioni, with his Italian breeding, was cautious. He glanced lightly from one to the other, and then drooped his eyelids. Ménard and Barry exchanged a long look. The look was nervous, a plea for mutual

The Call of the Talent

assistance and backing, like two ships in distress running up signals.   Signals for what?

That the two understood one another was evident, they two by themselves. All the others, including myself, were puzzled. But one fact was certain. The distress and the interest were all for one person. From the first moment of entering the studio, during the dinner, afterward, no matter who spoke, what story was told, they were all side issues. It was curious, unaccountable; but the man who spoke least, who had told nothing, it was he all through who had held the stage, unwillingly, unconsciously, who was never for a single second forgotten. The pivot about which we all turned was Travis.

As this conviction, which had taken root early in the evening, deepening, strengthening, flashed suddenly full-grown as the truth before me, I met Barry's eye. He looked at me squarely. Without words, without signs, the significance there was the same that had passed between him and the Doctor. I was startled, nonplussed. What did they want of me? It was just as a land-lubber standing on shore, watching two seamen. The flags, the signals, run up, run down, eagerly, frantically—they meant nothing at all. The longer he watches, the more they confuse him. My temper began to rise all at once; my eyes flashed back. As Barry saw this he made a swift motion.

"What the devil, Whittemore!" I exclaimed. "Look out for your foot! What do you mean by kicking me under the table?"

"Sh-h, McD.— sh-h!"

The others looked around.

"I beg your pardon," said Barry curtly.

"Did you want anything?" I retorted with irritation. "Why don't you speak out plainly?"

He gave me a withering glance.

As he turned his shoulders, shrugging them, again I felt that slight nudge, gentle this time, more politic, yet not to be disregarded. Under the folds of the table-cloth a boot lay wedged against mine.

"What the dev——"

Before the words were out of my mouth the Doctor's hand gripped my arm. My anger died in a flash. His voice was casual, his manner indifferent, but he gripped me so that it hurt.

"Eh, what, Doctor?" To my surprise I found myself stammering. "Did you speak? Excuse me!"

"Yes," he said. "Yes, I did. Nothing important." He stooped and struck a match. "Nothing of any consequence. It was only a matter of definition, the definition of talent.

The Call of the Talent

What it is, what it leads to. That's in your line,
sir; isn't it? It's a subject that interests me
greatly. There must be heaps of talent running
waste in Paris. That story of Nicot's started me
thinking."

I stared at him in surprise. "Why, yes," I
said, "there is; plenty of waste, of course!"

My answer, unwilling at first, churlish, seemed
to arouse the Doctor's interest. I prolonged it
in response to the question in his gaze. "Yes,
sir, out of a thousand so-called talents studying
here to-day one art or another in this great art
metropolis— it's a rough guess of course, but I
doubt if a percentage of more than ten succeeds."

"Wins out, you mean?"

"Wins out, makes good, whatever you choose
to call it. Most of them go under."

"Why?"

I laughed and shrugged my shoulders.

"Well, Doctor, in this world talent, that is
mere facility, feeling, technique, even a strong
bent and call along a certain line, isn't enough.
There's got to be vitality, vitality of spirit and
brain, staying power besides. A grit to go through
hell if needs be, and very few have it. Talent is
like a germ. You can develop it, yes, up to a certain point; keep it under control in a test-tube if
necessary. But once out of the laboratory, the

227

result depends not so much on the germ as the person it happens to enter, the other germs it runs across—circumstances, in other words. It's circumstances, Doctor, that hold the reins with most talents."

Ménard nodded his head.

"You may be right," he said; "but in that case I don't know— how is it with genius? Do circumstances control that too? If only grit is necessary, look at the countless number of art students here, slaving, starving, sacrificing every mortal thing in life to carry out their ends; and where do most of them come to? There must be more than we think, my friend, who go through hell for nothing. How do you explain that?"

"You can't explain it, Doctor, except as I just told you. For years now I have known this studio life in Paris, known it down to the ground, went through it myself. Why the struggle for barest existence, the breath to use the talent they have, in more cases than you dream of is enough to make one shudder. Given health, backing, a friend or two, a little encouragement, a fair wind in short, and they pull through to their goal. Without these—I am speaking now of the great majority, gentlemen, and what I say I know— the backing fails, the health gives out, indifferent friends, discouragement, a squall or two and a

The Call of the Talent

rough sea, and over goes the boat—the talent shipwrecked, dashed to atoms on the reefs, and that's all."

"Curious thing!" said Barry. "What on earth makes them do it? I go around with McD. to these studios, and watch the students at work. Some are young, some are old, some have great talent and some have very little, but they all daub away with the same ecstatic expression. Great Scott! The hours spent in slaving over those easels, the same zeal and devotion, would bring them in a good living in any other profession. Isn't that so, Doctor?"

Ménard was smoking dreamily. He tapped the ash off his cigar with the tip of his little finger and threw a glance at the Niké.

"I don't think so," he said; "no. When I was a young practitioner and first settled in Paris, I used to feel as you do; but now, after years of experience in dealing with just such cases, story after story and tragedy after tragedy, I've gained a great respect for the motive power behind them. That's a natural law, the call of the talent. There's a reason for it, gentlemen."

"How is that, Doctor?" Barry and I both exclaimed simultaneously; and the others, excepting Travis, all joined in, listening. Ménard smoked on in silence for a moment.

The Bachelor Dinner

"In these days of nerve diseases, gentlemen, you know that's my specialty—neurasthenia, exhaustion of the tissues, prostration, all the different forms from brain fag to madness—I've studied the trend, the conditions pretty closely; they mostly come from one cause."

"What?"

"Lack of outlet. Something's clogged up that ought to have its way. Like a machine intended for a certain kind of pins; feed it, put in another sort, and it soon gets out of order. Nothing fits; the gear's wrong. Keep on, and you'll smash it. The machine itself is all right, the fault is with the running. Given an intricate mechanism put together for a purpose, and change that purpose afterward— you follow me, gentlemen?"

"Not exactly," said Barry.

Ménard took his cigar out and shifted it.

"A man came to me the other day, a successful merchant. He had a huge business, inherited from his father. Everything was going well; no debts, no skeletons. The man was a nervous wreck.

'What's the matter with me, Doctor?' he said. 'I'm all gone to pieces!'

I examined him from foot to head. Organically he was sound; and he sat there all in a tremble, with his rudder loose to the wind.

The Call of the Talent

'Matter with you?' I said. 'You're trying to keep a fire alight when the grate is choked with ashes. It won't burn, it can't. There isn't any draught.'

'Draught?' he exclaimed, blinking.

'Yes, my friend. Underneath there, out of sight, the ashes have been piling up, piling up for years. You thought the wood was green or the match was damp, didn't you? Well, they're not! It's only the ashes, and you've got to shovel them off.'

'Are you crazy, Doctor?'

'No,' I said; 'but you'll be if you don't get out that shovel.'

Gentlemen, that man had started life with a very strong bent, a passion for the study of science. I knew him as a boy. We went through the Lycée Henri Quatre together. They expected great things of him. Then, in the midst of his training, the last year in the Sorbonne, his elder brother died, the one who was partner with his father in the business. The father was an old man and he had no other sons. There was nothing else for it. It nearly broke the fellow's heart; but he threw up his career, the career he was made for, and stepped into the breach. From that moment on the tread-mill never stopped. He was twenty-five when it hap-

The Bachelor Dinner

pened, fifty-five when he came to me. All his inner cravings, his ambition for those thirty years, had been boiling and seething like a whirlpool inside of him, dammed up by circumstances.

All that stress and strain and nerve-wear for success in a business that he wasn't fitted to run, that he didn't care a straw for. The money pleased his wife, a fool—meant a peaceful, contented old age for the father, legacies for the children, enough probably to ruin them. Oh yes, as a business man he carried the thing to the top notch, he did his duty thoroughly. And the ashes piled up! I tell you, gentlemen—" The Doctor flung his cigar down fiercely on the table half smoked, still lighted. "When you see these people with their nerves all gone to smash, there's a reason for it always. The longer I practise, the more I'm convinced of it. There's got to be an outlet! You dare not trifle with the instincts inside of you."

"That's true enough," said Barry. "Doctor, my experience in law bears out what you say. Most of the troubles in life, physical as well as mental, come from just that—the square peg in the round hole, going against nature. But still that doesn't explain (to go back to the art students, Doctor) what drives that rabble in hordes here to Paris; the rabble without talent, or pre-

The Call of the Talent

cious little of it. They slave and starve and go through hell just as the others, but if there's a spark of the real thing in them— You needn't shake your head, McD.! I haven't been watching these misguided young people, copying all these years in the Louvre, for nothing. Divine fire burning in those crazy-heads? Jove! You'd have to fetch your X-rays to locate it, Doctor!"

Barry's eyes sparkled. He laughed and looked at Ménard. The Doctor glanced at me.

"As to that," he said quickly, "the art side of the question I leave to the artist. Have the students really talent or not? That's for him to answer. My part, my experience, is with the medical side. If you want to know the real truth of the matter, Mr. Whittemore"—he spoke with a certain roughness—"art, all the arts, music, literature, sculpture, painting—they have a certain function, scope, unrealized by many, which gives dignity, a *raison d'être* to their pursuit apart from mere beauty, or the pleasure that beauty gives: the cult of the ideal. It is this that makes them sacred, and without it they are nothing. Gentlemen—" Ménard stopped a moment, took up his cigar again thoughtfully, relighted it.

"I am talking of art now, you understand, the real thing, not of modern excrescences. Mr. McD., if he exhibits in the Salon, will excuse me. There

233

The Bachelor Dinner

are instances in life, moments, moods, when something drives us mad—like a horse with blind-staggers whirling round and round. You have felt it, I have felt it. Something ugly, naked, brutal, that rises up before us. A sudden truth, a reality that strikes you full in the face, that sucks you down like an undertow from which there is no escaping.

When this stark moment comes, for some natures, peculiarly those sensitive, gifted, whether they have the mechanical skill or not, art and what it stands for is the only safety-valve. In it they find the ideal, the beautiful, that they have sought in vain in real life. In it they forget themselves. Their own fate, their own curse, seem petty in its presence. So they join the crowd of acolytes. Not the priests of art, mind! They have no call to approach the high altar except as humble servitors. The sacraments are not for them. To ring the bell, to swing the incense, to light the candles, that is their function and that is all they ask— the freedom of the temple.

Gentlemen," said Ménard, "for twenty years now I have watched over these art students that pour into Paris, attended them in their illnesses, helped them through their hard times, listened to their secrets. This matter is a hobby of mine, done sub rosa, and very few guess it. I don't

The Call of the Talent

want them to guess it, but what I say to-night I know." His hand crashed down on the table.

"Given a man or a woman, young, brought face to face with some sudden horror. They are dazed at first, paralyzed, numbed; then nature recoils. Like a rushing mountain torrent with a rock flung into its path, it beats against the obstacle, foams, tosses in vain. After a little the pressure of the water, finding itself blocked, its force always increasing, drives over the pebbles, through the earth, the underbrush, churning out a new stream-bed. The rock has hurled it from the path. Very good; it seeks another. The other, for many of these students, leads to Paris. That very zeal, absorption, that you speak of, Mr. Whittemore"—Ménard turned to Barry—"is the torrent fighting the rock. And God help it, I say! Whether the new stream-bed be the right track or not, God help it for its pluck!"

The Doctor's voice was husky. He covered his face with his hand suddenly, as if shutting out some memory, and sat there lost in thought. In the silence that followed, whether from telepathy or what, I don't know, but Barry motioned to me.

"Tell about it, McD., tell about it," he urged. "The Doctor hit the nail on the head that time, didn't he?"

"What?"

The Bachelor Dinner

"Why, the case of that young student. You remember, don't you—several months ago? The one who was in Moor's studio."

I nodded back.

It was rather odd. From the moment that the Doctor had begun talking, throughout the whole discussion, the remembrance of that student affair had been haunting me, hammering through my brain like an *idée fixe*. A curious experience, past and gone long before, one among many others that had left a deep impression. It was Ménard's voice that had raised the echo. Instinctively, impulsively, I turned to him and answered.

"If you really want to hear the story, Doctor? What Barry says is true; it illustrates your point in rather a vivid fashion. An odd case, a mysterious one, which I happened to run across personally."

Ménard looked up, dropping his hand with a start. I may have been mistaken, but his face had a flushed, moved look, his eyes a certain brilliance, almost as if— They rested full on Travis.

"Yes, yes," he said. "Go ahead! I'd like to hear the experience."

His voice sounded dreamy, as if absorbed in something else; but the tone was one of authority,

The Call of the Talent

the authority of the specialist, who out of pure courtesy, conceding perhaps to the wish of the patient's friends, has asked an opinion from another practitioner—the case being his own, knowing it from A to Z, the whys and wherefores as no outsider could. That at least was my impression, intensified by the absent-mindedness, the emotion of his manner. Hurriedly, averting my gaze I began.

"It was early in September that the incident happened, gentlemen. You all know Moor's studio?"

"The great Moor on the Rue Bonaparte?"

"The great Moor, yes. He has a few pupils, not very many. The greatest living painter in oils to-day; and to get up those dark back stairs to his work-shop has been the dream of every student at the Beaux-Arts for the last generation. The *Prix de Rome* runs it a close race; but personally, to my mind, that little bandy-legged man has the Villa Medici beaten to nothing! He takes only those he will; and he teaches without pay, for sheer love of his art. Very few ever get beyond the second turn of the staircase, still fewer open the door. But of those who are once inside and under the master's eye, a bare handful, sometimes less, the names have been mostly famous. No money, no influence, no ropes of any

The Bachelor Dinner

kind can help a student there. With genius they can enter, without genius they can't. What he has is the pick of Paris. . . . You know the master, Doctor?"

Ménard started.

"Who— Moor? Why, yes—yes, I know him!"

"Do you know him well?"

"Rather."

As the Doctor spoke, he slipped his hand in his breast-pocket and drew out a fresh cigar, breaking the label carelessly.

"My last, my Havana! I like to smoke it just at the end before going back to work. There's another where this came from. . . . Want to try it, Dan?"

Travis made no answer.

"Dannie!"

Ménard leaned forward with anxiety in his voice, peering into the dusk. Then as the silence continued, he sank back again in his chair, motioned to me to go on. The sudden question, the movement, senseless as they seemed, were evidently prompted by panic. Was the outline in the corner Travis, or only a shadow? Had he disappeared or not? As the Doctor relaxed, I took my cue and proceeded.

"If you know Moor— The reason I asked you was this. Any one who knows Moor well has heard of this eccentricity. He hates women like the devil itself, and he won't have one in his studio."

"I've heard that!" said Nicot.

"Yes?... Well, all the students find it out as soon as they get to Paris. The ambition to paint in Moor's studio, attacks them like a fever, women and men alike, before they've fairly crossed the court-yard of the Beaux-Arts. The summit, the end, the goal of all their strivings! A man with real genius, provided always it's the quantity and quality Moor wants, has a fighting chance to win. A woman, no matter what she has, never! That's a law immutable as the laws of the Medes and Persians; and has never, to the knowledge of the art students, been broken."

Ménard gave me a quick glance.

"But there's no use telling you all this, Doctor. If you know Moor, you know it already. He's a wonderful teacher."

We all sat and smoked for a little in silence. The breeze caught the yellow curtains, blowing them to and fro; the door above swayed again, creaking on its hinges. As it did so, Travis stirred.

"Go on," cried Barry hurriedly, "go on, McD! Tell them about that afternoon in the studio. The time——"

The Bachelor Dinner

"The time when Moor——"

"Yes, the day he——"

"Well, the way that came about," I exclaimed, "was natural enough. I had gone there to consult about the arrangement of our exhibit, some special things for the autumn Salon. We were both on the committee; and I found Moor in his velvet coat with a group of students working—seven young men scattered in different corners, all intent on their canvases; and Moor strolling in and out, a pipe in his mouth, a watchful look in his eye, stopping here, there in his walk to bend over an easel. He came forward at once to meet me. At the first glimpse of the students, naturally I did my best to escape.

'No, no' he said, 'come! You're just the man I want, McD. Come along here with me and see what these fellows are doing.'

Moor hooked his arm in mine and pulled me along beside him.

'Give a good look around and let me know your opinion.' He whispered this in my ear, pressing my arm for silence. 'There's a reason for it, McD.,' he said, 'so keep your eyes open.'

We made the rounds together.

Talk about talent, Doctor! Why those seven men in that studio had more talent between them than I've ever seen painting under one roof be-

The Call of the Talent

fore. The work was something superb. I said as much to Moor, in an undertone of course, but scarcely able to repress my enthusiasm. We went from easel to easel. The master kept my arm in his, pressing it from time to time, as if to remind me of the students' presence. As I studied the canvases, each in turn, suddenly it flashed through my mind, extraordinary as it seemed, that Moor himself was studying me.

In spite of his careless manner, a certain pride, natural enough, that the gardener who waters such rare plants must necessarily feel toward their blossoming, there was a note of anxiety, irritation in his gesture; almost as if such spontaneous exclamations of delight had disappointed him, as if in some way from me he had expected something else. Inconceivable as it sounds, I felt this in the atmosphere; even the students felt it. They painted on steadily and never turned their heads, never raised an eyelash. At the last one, unmistakably Moor's frown was deeper, his manner moody, impatient, almost rude. I stood in silence, examining the canvas.

'Well, McD., have you finished?'

'Yes,' said I regretfully.

'Then come along with me, come into my den! I want to talk, away from these fellows, out of sight where they won't hear!'

The Bachelor Dinner

Moor whispered this hurriedly, still dragging at my arm. I followed him into the back room, a queer, shabby little place, with canvases about and a skylight; evidently for work, not show, and not open to cleaners. Flinging a painting-cloth from a chair, he motioned me down, leaning his arm on an easel. His manner was rather odd.

'Well, McD.— well?'

'I congratulate you, maître.'

'Future exhibitors, eh? Sacrement!... Make rather a fine showing, don't they?'

My response was full of enthusiasm.

Moor lifted one shoulder, with that expressive, wordless shrug which says so much from a Frenchman.

'Temperament, talent, capacity for work—it's all there,' he said. 'Every man in that studio is specially picked and chosen, and each one has a future before him. If he hadn't, out he'd go! I'm working for the building of a better art, McD., laying corner-stones in fact; and it isn't worth my while to bother with any chipped blocks. They've got to be whole and perfect. The kind I want, too!'

'Mon Dieu, maître, they all look it!' I cried.

'Yes,' said Moor; 'I think they do, I think they do. When I've once made a choice I'm rarely disappointed; but'— he spoke slowly as if weighing his words—'as you went over the canvases, McD., from one to the other, you noticed the students perhaps. You didn't happen to mark any particular one, did you?'

'Why yes, I noticed two.'

'So!'

'The thin chap with reddish hair, who was doing a portrait from memory. His hand was as steady as any master's and the skill of the likeness extraordinary. There wasn't a false line or tone in the entire composition.'

'Hm-m,' said Moor; 'that's Louis Fabre. Going in for portraits. Very chic talent and a good jaw. He'll succeed. . . . Any other?'

Again I noticed that note of irritation in his voice.

'Why yes, the one in the corner. The little dark-eyed fellow who was working on that landscape. A mountain lake at night, dark, lonely, you remember? with the mist creeping over the water and a boat floating bottom upward. The way he painted that creeping mist, the gloom, the suspense made me shiver. Done from memory too, was it?'

'Either that,' said Moor, 'or evolved from some inner consciousness. This class has no models. It's creative work I'm after. Any fool machine can copy, and machines are out of my line. So

The Bachelor Dinner

that dark-eyed little fellow is the best you think, McD.?'

Moor gave me a sharp look.

'Yes,' I said decidedly; 'if you want my opinion. There was something so striking, so emotional about that painting, in the conception, feeling, atmosphere. For a boy as young as that to wield so strong a brush, he must be unusually gifted, maître, even for one of your following.'

'Oh, he's gifted all right,' said Moor; 'he's gifted. Works like a galley slave and poor as poverty. Handsome fellow too. Pity he's so slim, undersized, has a hand like a girl's.' Again his eyes seemed to question me.

'So many of the students are like that,' I said. 'Scant food, long hours, exposure! What else do you expect? Young, alone, half-starved, full of dreams, left to shift for himself. Isn't that about the tale? From his eager look, his pallor, I sized him up at a glance. There are thousands of others just like him in Paris, only without the genius. The talents go under where the genius pulls through. This one at any rate is all right, maître. There's been hell enough in his past, judging from the look of him; but now that he's in your hands——'

'Well?' said Moor suddenly.

'Well, that spells success, fame, doesn't it?

244

The Call of the Talent

Isn't your name the key, the open sesame to the art world?' I laughed. 'Any pupil of yours— all Paris knows that, maître— goes from your doorstep to a pretty certain future.'

'They do,' said Moor, 'if they get that far, if they're not pitched out first.'

'What?' I cried. 'Heavens! You don't mean that boy, Moor?'

'I do.'

'You would pitch out a student with genius like that! Why, what for? What on earth? What's the fellow done?'

'Genius or no genius,' said Moor roughly, 'I'll pitch him out neck and crop, and what's more, this very day.' He brought his hand down with a crash against the easel. 'That's why I asked you to stay here, McD. If it hadn't been for the genius he'd have gone long ago—that and being a poor devil. Poor, McD.— mon Dieu! If that fellow has more than a dry crust for his dinner most nights, I'd be surprised. He lives on a mere nothing. And he's stark mad for the brushes, he cares for nothing else.'

'Then why, why on earth——'

'It's a damned disagreeable business!' Moor broke out passionately. 'To tell you the truth, McD., ever since I've known the thing, and it's some time now, I've been trying my best to lash

245

The Bachelor Dinner

myself up to it. The fact is, when you came in
to-day— Lord, the relief it was to see you! Now
for the leap, I said to myself. We'll settle the
job, get it over!'

As Moor said this, gentlemen, his face was white
with rage. He kept twiddling his fingers, and
his whole frame quivered. If you know the
master, Doctor, you know how he is in a temper?"

Ménard gave a dry laugh.

"Why his nerves were so on edge, tense, I could
almost have sworn he was frightened!

'Leap to what?' I cried. 'Do what? Settle
what? . . . Moor, for heaven's sake, explain!'

'You didn't see for yourself then, McD.?'

'Anything wrong, you mean?'

'Anything wrong with that little dark-eyed
chap?'

'No, no—I didn't!'

'You're blind, man!' he exclaimed, 'blind as a
bat! So was I for a long while. Couldn't you
see, couldn't you tell? Why that dark-eyed boy
is a——'

As Moor stopped, our eyes met. A sudden
light flashed across me. The boy's face came back
as he had bent over the easel—his dark curls
against the low collar, the white of his throat
showing beneath it, the slim, stooping form, the
eyes intent, the small hand with the brush.

The Call of the Talent

There was that so picturesque, absorbed about him, so high strung, so unusual, I had marked him at once out of all the others, even apart from his canvas.

'You don't mean,' I cried, 'not——'

Moor nodded grimly.

Before I could finish my sentence, he had rushed to the door, opened it and called out. The next moment the boy stood before us. Absurdly young and small he seemed, his dark eyes dreamy, the brush still clasped in his fist.

'Shut the door,' said Moor sharply. 'Shut the door and bolt it. Now, sir, come over here. What the devil do you mean by palming yourself off as a——'

The boy leaped back as if he'd been struck.

'Deny it, will you— eh?' cried Moor, his temper getting the best of him. 'Eh, will you?' He shook his fist in the boy's face. 'Do you think we're fools, do you think we don't know? Sacré! You're a woman!'

As this accusation burst from Moor's lips, we three alone in that spooky bare little studio—it was an awful moment, gentlemen. I shall never forget it, never! In the silence that followed, intense, ghastly, you could have heard our three hearts beating. For a second the boy stood stock-still. He was trembling like an aspen. Then

The Bachelor Dinner

the door on the staircase swung back with a slam. Moor and I were alone. The shock cooled his anger at once.

'My God, he's gone, McD.! Gone! Do you hear? And hasn't even confessed! I meant to pitch him out, yes; but not like that! Not like that!'

Between the rage and the worry Moor was almost frantic.

'I only meant to confront him, McD. You know how I hate women. I won't have the creatures around, and to have one in here disguised—no, no! Genius or not, I won't have it! I won't have it! But you go after him, McD., go after him. I haven't the remotest idea where he lives; and he's poor—we mustn't lose sight of him.'

I dashed away down the staircase.

Now, gentlemen, as I told you, all this happened some time ago. From that day to this, Moor has hunted, I have hunted, we have ransacked all the art quarters, the Beaux-Arts, the private studios, questioned all the students, set detectives on the track; but the boy or woman, whichever it is, has vanished right out of Paris."

Ménard looked up with interest.

"Sure you weren't mistaken?"

"No, I don't think so, Doctor. Of course my own impressions were fleeting enough, but Moor

The Call of the Talent

was perfectly positive. If not, why did the fellow flee?"

"That's so," said Ménard, "that's so. Queerer things have happened. For a woman alone in Paris, especially for an art student, to pose as a boy would be a safeguard; at least she probably thought so, particularly with beauty. And then, as you say, it's the only way that a woman could enter Moor's studio."

"Exactly. That was the trouble."

"Done for the sake of her art, then! They're a reckless lot, those students, when the call of the talent is strong. Moor never heard what happened?"

"No, we couldn't trace her. When you asked a while ago, Doctor, how it was with genius, if circumstances controlled that too, I thought of that dark-eyed student, half-starving, dead perhaps, or painting alone in some garret. The thought has haunted me ever since. But the strangest part of the whole thing was, what first made Moor suspicious.

'McD.,' he said, 'do you know that boy had been six months here in the studio. For the greater part of the time he was taking in fuel, just as they all have to; doing studies in black and white to correct some fault in his lines. Then the whole class, having reached about the same point, stretched

The Bachelor Dinner

their canvases, got their oils and palettes out, and started to work on composition. That was a fortnight ago. The subjects were left open, my usual method. They blocked out freely, each one, as all my students do, what their creative instincts dictated, what their inner fancies saw. From the choice as well as the handling I can tell what stuff they're made of. You noticed the force of that landscape? Well, it was that, that struck me directly.

In my opinion, McD., there are two kinds of talent, of the head and of the heart. The former, originating in the brain, dependent on the intellect and its development, goes far. It is like a rock stratum with veins of gold shot through it, running here, there, in all directions, to be followed, worked, claimed as long as the ore holds out. Men who have talent at all, I have found, generally belong to this type, although of course with exceptions. But the heart talent is different. That is fed from some inner spring deep down in the nature, dependent almost entirely on feelings, emotions, passions that have had no other vent. Block up the spring and it bursts forth in a flood. The power is something terrific; but deceptive, McD.— deceptive. It is like a mine that is soon shut down. No strata there, no veins, no ore. What you've gained is a single nugget.

The Call of the Talent

Now the moment I saw that landscape, 'This is no casual imagining,' I said, 'no sober brain conception, either of thought or memory. It's something less and it's something more. Is that boy painting with oils? No! It's his own heart's blood. Odd thing that, in a man,' I thought, 'especially such a young one. Never ran across such a thing before in all my years spent with students!' From that time on I noted the boy closer, watched him at work, saw how he handled both his subject and his brushes.

The intensity of it, the absorption, the feverish, head-over-heels, devil-may-care unconsciousness of the body—what it ate, what it drank, ill or well, strong or feeble. His indifference, not only to the world outside, but to the studio itself and the students. Was that a boy painting? All the forces and needs of his nature lavished out on a single nugget? 'Never!' I said. 'Impossible! There's not a boy in the world who would do it, no matter what his hell had been, no matter what he'd lived through.' And then, McD., the thought once launched, I soon jumped to conclusions.

That is a woman, my friend, no boy! A woman whose talent is like a horse without a check-rein, the harness broken, the shafts smashed, careering madly ahead. And now,' groaned Moor, 'I've

turned her out, I've turned her loose! Heaven
only knows what will come of it! McD., I'd give
a thousand pounds if I'd kept my hand on the
bit!'

The poor maître! Those were his words exactly, repeated over and over. Since then, gentlemen, we've searched everywhere, advertised,
used every method imaginable, all without result.
Of course it's hopeless now. I've never seen Moor
so cut up, so worried to death over anything."

As I said this—there was a carafe of water on the
table—I poured out a glass and emptied it. The
others went on smoking. By this time the Doctor was half way through his Havana, and was
holding it up between his fingers, examining the
end with absorption. Whether calculating the
length of his rest-time left, or deep in some problem or other, I wondered but could not be sure.
He pondered so long and he sat so still the silence grew rather oppressive. For some reason,
it was curious—no one else seemed willing to break
it. The candles burned lower, the shadows grew
darker, and still not a word was spoken. A spell
was over the circle, as if we were waiting for something.

"Sacrement!" exclaimed the Doctor suddenly.
"Mon Dieu, if that isn't odd!"

"What?" We all started.

The Call of the Talent

"To be told that story to-night of all nights! Way back in September you say it happened, man— and you never knew? It's extraordinary!"

Ménard hesitated a moment; then he swung around in his chair all at once as if he'd reached some decision.

"Extraordinary!" he repeated. "Well, gentlemen, since the tale has been told thus far, I might as well finish it for you. One night last March the hospital had a hurry call. An American deaconess who is working here in Paris, calling on one of the art students in the quarter there by the *Halles*, had run across an emergency case—a fellow student raving, alone, in a garret under the leads. There was nothing in the garret but a mattress with one ragged blanket, a broken pitcher empty, an easel, a piece of canvas, a box of oils nearly gone, and two worn brushes. No water, no food, nothing else of any kind. The window-panes were broken, the snow and wind were in the room, and the cold was nearly zero. Across the mattress, delirious, huddled under the blanket— Heaven only knows how long it had lasted, but the deaconess, passing through the hallway outside, heard the sound of raving, came in and found that boy there. She sent word to the hospital, telephoned for me."

Again the Doctor hesitated.

The Bachelor Dinner

"I looked after the case, gentlemen. It was hit or miss, and it lasted for weeks; but at last we pulled him through."

"Him?" I exclaimed. "Moor was wrong, then!"

"No."

"What? You don't mean to say——"

"Moor was right," said Ménard, "perfectly right. The fact is, if you really want to know what became of——"

He adjusted his Havana, puffed once or twice, then waved his hand toward the gallery.

Mercedes 1104

WE were all so taken aback by this that we stared at the Doctor in amazement.

"What!" I cried. "That art student, boy—woman, I mean— she's up there? Your secretary, Doctor?"

"My secretary!" Ménard exclaimed. "N-no. That is—" He laughed rather nervously and lowered his voice.

"Well, yes; I call her that, I call her that! You see, gentlemen, when she came out of the hospital the child was like a ghost. Nothing to her so far as flesh goes; white, frail, transparent as alabaster. But as to spirit, mon Dieu! For sheer will-power, pride, determination, in all my life, in all my practice, in man, woman, or child, I've never seen its equal. She ought to have gone to the country, rested, done nothing for six months at least. I did my best to force it. But no— sacré! Since she had no money of her own, she wouldn't be beholden, and she'd either work or starve. Painting for a while was out of the question. Her tools and materials had all gone to the *Mont-de-Piété* with her other belongings.

255

The Bachelor Dinner

You can't paint long with a few half-empty oil tubes, a ragged piece of canvas and two worn brushes. And besides she hadn't the strength."

Ménard laughed again still more nervously. It was evident that he did so to keep himself in hand, to force down some emotion; for he turned his face away, smoking until the blue rings enveloped him like a cloud. Out of it, when he finally spoke, his voice sounded strange, almost smothered.

"So that's how it came about. We compromised, gentlemen. Travis had his laboratory rigged up here. He had just finished his— But there, I dare say not one of you has heard a word about it. He's a terrible chap for reserve, that fellow!... Why don't you own up, Dannie, eh?... This host of ours, my friends— To be sure, I'm a Frenchman and he's an American, but in science as in art there is, or there should be, no such thing as nationality. We're all brothers and we meet in the same field, so what I say, I say freely.

For five years now, Dan has been working here in Paris over a series of germ experiments so difficult, so dangerous that there isn't another investigator, either in his country or my own, who would dare to even attempt them. . . . There, Travis, there, man, you needn't say a word! I ought to know what I'm talking about!... Why,

256

gentlemen, the medical journals to-day are all full of his name. In all the vast fog-bank that stretches ahead of us doctors, that lies between us and knowledge, there isn't another pioneer, not another one, I tell you, who has done for research what he has."

The Doctor's eyes flashed, his voice rang out. Before any one could speak, he had leaped to his feet and was standing with both hands on Dan's shoulders; bending low over his chair as if, while drawing all eyes to that spot, instinctively, knowing his friend, he still wanted to shield him.

"Forgive me, Travis," he said, "forgive me! If you were left to yourself— you've the instincts of the mole, you know, to burrow underground. No one would ever hear of your work unless once in a while—" Ménard stammered, glanced around, then lowered his voice suddenly.

"To-night I had to speak out, Dan; just to-night. There's a reason."

Travis muttered something in a muffled voice; but with the Doctor between and the darkness, his face and expression were hidden. Their hands clasped; we could see nothing more. Then Ménard sank down beside him.

"Well, of all things!" cried Barry. "The deuce! Here McD. and I are his college mates, and we've never even known Dan's profession;

The Bachelor Dinner

not since our foot-ball days when he was captain
and led us a dance over the field. Brains, mas-
tery, grit, resource, he had them all then. We always imagined he'd set the world on fire, bring
fame to his alma mater. Why the whole college, professors, students, and all, were backing
him up to win, when— You see, Doctor, for
years now we've all lost sight of him. He vanished out of the Alumni Club, the fraternity life,
everything. I doubt if there's a man in the *Theta
Delt'* who dreams a word of this business! . . . I
say, old fellow, that isn't fair! Why on earth
have you kept so mum? Why didn't you tell
us, Travis?"

The sudden, ghastly silence that followed
tripped Barry up, brought him to a dead stop,
turned him white as a sheet. He gave one glance
at the shadow in the corner. It was like a battery
charged with a wireless message. You could see
nothing, you could hear nothing, yet the message
went straight to its goal.

"Oh!" said Barry hoarsely; his voice trembled. "Oh, er— by the way, Doctor, you didn't
finish your story. You were just in the midst
of telling us about that little woman up yonder;
how she happened to be your secretary. Jove!
Between McD.'s account and yours she must be
an interesting creature. Couldn't you bring her

down here, make some excuse or other? I must say for my own part, you've piqued my curiosity until it's all up on edge! How about the rest of you, gentlemen? Don't you feel the same way? Couldn't you manage somehow to give us a glimpse of her, Doctor—now, before it gets too late? We'll have to be going shortly."

He rattled all this off, hardly stopping for breath.

"No," said Ménard. "Sorry I can't!" His tone was low, rather curt. "She's in charge of an experiment of mine up there, and she wouldn't report before the time or show herself—not for a fortune! For heaven's sake, man, don't suggest such a thing. Hush, she might hear you! Besides——"

Here the Doctor's voice, hesitating, dropped down several tones. We all drew closer, cigars suspended, straining our ears to listen.

"Besides, er— to tell you the truth, that child up there, is really a married woman!"

"Married?" Barry exclaimed.

"Married, yes. It's a queer case. The fact of the matter is— Draw closer, gentlemen, I dare not speak loud. Why, the bottom reason for all that masquerading was— I wonder you didn't guess. She had run away from her husband."

The Bachelor Dinner

"Divorced you mean, Doctor?"

"No, not divorced, not separated, nothing legal about it. Just dropped her wedding-ring and ran."

"The devil!" said Barry. "What for? Didn't she love her husband?"

Ménard moved in his chair uneasily.

"Yes—yes, she loved him."

"Then why? That's odd. Perhaps he didn't love her?"

"Perhaps."

"Was that it?"

The Doctor said nothing for a moment or two. He held up his Havana, studied it. The end was shorter now, almost gone, but the tip of the ash burned brightly; the blue rings still encircled him.

"That was it, Mr. Whittemore—the conviction in her mind at least, strong enough at the time to drive her from him and to keep her from him to-day. Whether true or false, who knows? The result has been the same. Whether the shot was fired by the man's hand or her own, by fact or imagination, the track of that bullet through her heart has ploughed a wound so deep, it has left a terrible scar, a scar that won't heal, that can't. Never! Unless, until——"

"The conviction is proved to be a lie, you mean?" said Barry.

Mercedes 1104

"Exactly, Mr. Whittemore. But how are you going to prove a case when the facts are out of your hand? Those two are like some great rock, rent asunder by a lightning-stroke that has left a yawning chasm, deep, precipitous, terrible, with a torrent flowing between. The lightning struck straight and sharp, there's no delusion about it. Where the rock was one before, the stream divides it now. To reunite that rock again, to re-knit that jagged fissure, there's only the one way possible. The chasm has to be bridged. Gentlemen——"

Ménard laughed hoarsely. "My position tonight is that of a man facing that rock alone years after the storm broke; who sees the rent, who sees the precipice, who sees both sides and the torrent; whose mind dreams while his hands are bound. Without knowledge, without material, without a thing in the world to go on, how is the bridge to be built?"

As the Doctor said this he leaned forward, his voice tense, scarcely audible, gripping both arms of his chair.

"How, in God's name, is the bridge to be built, gentlemen? Answer me that question if you can, solve me that riddle—one of you, any of you, out of your experience of the world and its problems, personal or second hand, your own or another's.

The Bachelor Dinner

Help me, advise me! I've been racking my brains for weeks now and am still groping, undecided. Is there any feat of engineering, think you, that could span an arch across?"

The eagerness, the emotion in the Doctor's manner, half restrained until now, was unmistakable as he said this. That the matter was no mere passing interest, the natural protective instinct of the strong toward the weak, that craving to make the wrong right instinctive to some natures, but something more, something vital—not one of us there could doubt it. His eyes roved from face to face, repeating the question in silence. Startled, we all gazed back at him. No one answered the question, no one spoke for a moment. The tension began to grow oppressive.

It was Barry who broke it finally, knocking the ashes out of his pipe, with a sharp stroke against the hammered brass of the ash-tray. Then he spoke slowly, weighing his words, refilling his pipe as he did so.

"That storm, Doctor, that lightning-stroke you speak of, splitting the rock, causing the fissure, you know what started it, do you?"

"Yes."

"The usual thing?"

"The usual thing."

"That other woman—is she still alive?"

Mercedes 1104

"I don't know."

"Does the infatuation continue?"

"I don't know."

"Did it ever exist?"

"I don't know."

"That's exactly the point, Doctor. In my experience, nine cases out of ten, it never does exist or it's only a passing shadow. Nothing real, nothing true, nothing tangible about it; yet the shadow does the mischief." Barry spoke with emphasis. "If women understood this better! A man can play with fire, *will* play with it, an ignis fatuus, the sex in him akindle from the sex in some one else, all the while despising himself and the flame; his heart and his hearth through it all untouched, the one still sacred, the other still faithful. If women understood this better, I say, if the world understood it, and meddling, outside fools would only keep their hands off!"

Barry brought his fist down. All the pent-up feeling of the past, the self-reproach and the memory were in his voice and his gesture. His eyes sought a blotch in the darkness. In spite of the place, the strangers around, again he seemed pleading forgiveness. Why? Or was it imagination? Why should his thoughts so dwell on the past, why should mine? Dan, his long black shadow motionless, unresponsive, apparently took

The Bachelor Dinner

no notice. Silent, absorbed, dreaming, from first
to last he had held aloof, he had taken no part in
the evening; yet not for a moment, not for a
second— why was it we couldn't forget him?
Ménard broke out suddenly.

"As a matter of fact, have you ever met a case,
Mr. Whittemore, where, given the ignis fatuus,
given the flame, the hearth-fire has gone on burning?"

"Regardless, you mean—understanding?"

"Knowing the reason or guessing it, yes."

Barry pondered a moment.

"Not without fuel of some kind," he said;
"out of sheer love, no. For the sake of the children, if there are any, for money's sake, for respectability's sake, for the sake of the lookers-on,
the hearth in the drawing-room is often kept blazing, while the inner hearth is cold, dead ashes,
desolate. Poor comfort for a man who has slipped
to warm his hands by, especially if the slip was
false; a trick, a lie of circumstances all combined
to his undoing. That is the tragedy of many a
marriage, Doctor. If it is also the tragedy of that
little girl up there—" Barry pointed to the gallery. "Yet for all that, no matter what happens,
my own theory is, and I speak from some practical knowledge: where love has been once, no
matter what the storm, what the lightning-stroke,

how jagged the fissure, how deep and mad the torrent, the rock may be cleft and the chasm rent, but the span is always between, invisible, intangible, unsuspected often. It may be frail as a spider's web, or it may be strong as steel, but nature once united— it's one of our human mysteries, and all the arguments, all the dispensations, all the law courts in Christendom are rendered nil before it. No engineering will be necessary to build that bridge, Doctor, for the arch is already spanned; always has been, always will be, and no mortal power can break it."

Barry's face, still turned toward the blotch, was hidden; his voice rang out grimly, earnestly, with conviction, as a man reciting his creed. There was purpose, intention in every word he uttered; a fearless purpose, a curious intention, as if to force strong remedy on one who needed it sorely; to lance a wound that had gone too long festering, uncared for.

"Yes!" cried Barry. "Yes! The bridge is there, the rock is joined, still, always, in spite of everything. Silence, estrangement, death itself, even death, nothing alters——"

He faltered suddenly, stopped short. Travis had sprung to his feet. With his hand to his forehead in a dazed way, staring wide-eyed straight ahead of him, he began to pace up and down—not

The Bachelor Dinner

feverishly, not excitedly, but with a strange, mechanical stride, like that of a caged animal who knows from striking against them where the bars shut him in; hopeless, despairing of breaking through, his frenzy already spent, unconscious even of motion.

So Dan's movements seemed to us all. The Doctor watched him intently. At the fifth round he began to come to himself, almost as a sleep-walker; regaining with a start, a shock, consciousness of his surroundings, the sense of his own identity. His mind was evidently fixed, gripped fast by something Barry had said. One point, and one alone, had pierced like a barbed arrow through the mist of his own brooding. All the rest had fallen unheeded. Still pacing up and down restlessly, his head bent, with a weariness in his posture, a passion in his voice that none of us will ever forget, Travis confronted the Doctor.

"You asked a question a moment ago, Ménard, and Barry here answered it, out of his own experience as a man and as a lawyer. His answer was wrong, gentlemen—wrong, as most of us are when we try to limit human nature by what we know of it ourselves. There is always more to learn; there will always be exceptions. Since the world began, we men have made fools, knaves of ourselves, run after other flames, deserted our own hearth-stones; and as the outer flame flared up the inner fire burned low. Serves us right that it should. We deserve nothing better. We deserve that the fire should go out and leave us cold, kneeling before it conscience-smitten, shivering, full of horror, striving in vain to kindle a spark where dead ashes alone remain. Women are right in that, just; we can't blame them. They hitch their wagon to a star. The star falls to the dung heap. Should they follow and grovel too? Soil their hands, stain their garments, exchange for manure their own ether?"

Travis' face was white as chalk; it shone out in the darkness. His voice was low, but it bit like a lash, strained, tense, full of torment.

"So far, Barry, you're right, you're right. It needs fuel of a different kind if the hearth's to be kept going! 'For the sake of the children, if there are any, for money's sake, respectability's sake, the sake of the lookers-on; and sometimes'— good God!—'sometimes not even then! For sheer love, never!' . . . Never? You think that, do you? You're sure?"

Travis threw back his head and laughed, laughed long, strangely, terribly; a laugh that chilled our blood.

"God! So you think that? I used to myself long ago. Women, to my mind, were all in the

The Bachelor Dinner

same class, the same since the world began. A man may forge, steal, murder, have his portrait in the rogues' gallery, commit all the crimes in the calendar, and the woman will stick to him, true as steel. Most of them do; they always have. If he drinks and abuses her, it makes no difference. If he drives her out with oaths and blows on a cold winter night, with a little new-born babe in her arms, she returns in the morning. If the court has him up for breaking her head and commits him for assault, she will give her last penny to bail him out, and rend the magistrate tooth and nail for putting him there. Any Irish laundress who washes your shirts, any French cocotte from the Paris streets is capable of that. Yes, even the street-woman! Why, for what reason, heaven only knows! God bless her for it! But let a man make a certain misstep along a certain road, all others being open, and only this one closed——"

Travis stopped all at once. His pallor was ghastly. Again he passed his hand over his forehead, his eyes, as though caught in the web of some recollection, trying vainly to escape from it.

"Once, only once! No matter how short the step, how slight the distance may be. When he turns to go back, the way is barred to his feet, a gate slams in his face. The game is up, the play is out. She flees from him as from the plague!"

Mercedes 1104

Dan's voice was hoarse, rough. He went on with increasing bitterness.

"The one unforgivable sin! And no wonder, gentlemen, no wonder. Don't think I am taking the part of the man. He's earned what he's got; he deserves nothing better. Only once in a while, once in a hundred thousand years, there's a woman who understands—who, in spite of this, in spite of the worst, having no children, caring nothing for money, less for respectability, snapping her fingers at the lookers-on—for no reason at all save for sheer love, lives with him, dies with him, sticks to him from the sky to the gutter, through better and worse, through heaven and hell; and a woman like that— well, I met one once!" said Travis. "A strange experience, the strangest thing you ever heard. The thought of it has been in my mind all day, years ago though it happened. Gentlemen, for the life of me I can't shake it off. I might as well tell you about it."

He was still pacing up and down, the shadow full on his face. The atmosphere was cloudy, the smoke from the cigars like a mist rising, mysterious, as though shrouding some secret. Outside in the garden a wind had sprung up; it swept over the trees. The branches fretted and soughed against the blinds. From the distance came the rumble of thunder.

The Bachelor Dinner

"Yes," said Travis heavily, "to-night some-how, I don't know why, but the memory seems to obsess me. Both the man and the woman were old friends of mine; and the fate that overtook them the most tragic, the most terrible that could happen to any one. You will all say that. There are no two opinions. And yet, believe it or not as you like, by my soul it's the truth! I have envied those two, and always shall to my dying day, more than any one else in the world!"

He flushed as he said this, then went on hurriedly.

"The man was Perry Fabian. Perhaps you have heard of him, perhaps you haven't. The case made a stir when it happened."

"Perry Fabian, the sculptor, you mean?" Barry gave an exclamation.

"Yes, yes," Travis answered, still pacing, without turning his head. "That's the man, yes. You knew him then, did you?"

"Not personally, only by reputation and what the newspapers said."

"The newspapers? . . . What!"

Dan turned on his heel suddenly, sharply, and came to a dead standstill.

"Damn the newspapers! You believed what you read in them, did you? You a lawyer, a newspaper man once yourself! The harpies! The

270

Mercedes 1104

vampires! They surrounded that fine fellow, gossiped about him, lied about him, bandied his name from column to column, slung mud at it, drove him clean mad with their hints and innuendoes, sucked his life-blood fairly, and drove him to his death. They've done it to many a man before, many a woman. Once they get their teeth in, once their claws take hold! Oh, they're sly about it, they know the ropes, they keep within the law. They kill his reputation first. That's easy in our country. There's no escape, there's no redress. The escutcheon once blotted, the breast-plate torn away, the soul behind it quivering, bared for the hawks of the press to feed on— it may be true or it may be false, but the taint of it spreads like a poisonous wind, north, south, east, west, the length and breadth of the continent. To deny or refute it is hopeless! To deny, to refute is to rub it in, to give fresh impetus to a wind becalmed, to play the trump right into their hands." Travis crashed his fist down.

"Like a lot of flapping vultures hovering over a battle-field. Wherever they spy a human form down, forsaken, defenceless, watch them poise and swoop. Damn the newspapers, I say! To hell with the whole lot of them!"

He walked over to the window and stood a moment, looking down. The storm was increasing,

The Bachelor Dinner

the thunder coming nearer. A loose spray of
the clematis blew across his face; it fell with
a shower of drops. As it touched him, Travis
shrank instinctively, unconsciously. The gesture
of a man whose past has had some shock, lived
through long since, lived down; but whose nerves,
hard-pressed, overstrung, on edge, like a violin's
strings left too long on the pegs, will break at the
slightest strain. Dan gave a sudden start, drew
back. Then, as no one moved or broke the silence, he steadied his voice and went on.

"Fabian, gentlemen, if he had lived in the six-
teenth century, would have been a hard-working,
single-hearted, simple-living artist, with the tastes
and ideals of his class. No saint, for none of
them were, but he would have amounted to something. In the twentieth, his tastes expanded, his
ideals went to smash, and he flowed right along
with the current. Portrait busts were his specialty. He began doing creative work his first
years out of the atelier. But copying your neighbor in the street is much easier; the commonplace,
called realism, pays much better. Imagination
dies still-born in such surroundings, so you really
can't blame him.

They lived in a fashionable circle; one of
those gay suburban settlements outside of New
York, where the houses are expensive, automo-

Mercedes 1104

biles are plentiful, and the country club, with its polo, golf, and bridge-whist, is the centre. It was Perry who liked the gayety. His wife was a quiet, sober, nun-like little person, whose talents and attractions, for her own good and peace of mind, were also four centuries late; who no more fitted in, than an old-fashioned wild rose in a modern florist's window, or brown bread at a banquet. He went the pace and she stayed home, and no one knew much about her.

Perry golfed, poloed, bridged; flew from his home to New York in his big red touring Mercedes, from New York to his home and back again; wore a flower in his button-hole, led all the social functions, and sculptured his busts between times. The handsomest fellow, the most popular, and the man who did the least with his talent of any one I ever saw; the least, that is, except for money. He made plenty of that; too much. No art has ever survived that test, and his went under directly.

Bah!" said Travis. "Those busts of his! Simpering, vapid, overdressed women—done because they could pay the bill, or their husbands paid it for them. Poor Perry! A fool, of course! I used to warn him. And yet, no matter what he did, how angry he made you, what crimes against art his busts were, you couldn't help forgiving

The Bachelor Dinner

him, you couldn't help liking him. He was such a gay, warm-hearted fellow. Whether his wife expostulated or whether she left him alone, I often used to wonder. Money was nothing to her, society was less. She came of an artist family and had lived her youth in Italy. She knew what his busts were worth, and she knew his capabilities. She also knew her own power, and this was nil; at least so we thought at the time. At any rate, however that was, there was no effect apparent. Perry's artistic temperament, thriving in such conditions, soon overshadowed his talent. The one shot up like a weed while the other lay fallow; and as his portrait busts multiplied the neighbors began to talk. The reason was— it was none of their business, but the busts were all of one person."

Travis paced on, his head bent, his eyes on the ground, his brows drawn and moody.

"It's a curse of a thing to have," he said, "that temperament, so-called, of the artist. A necessary evil, like poison in some strong medicine. Without it the remedy is void; too much and the dose is fatal. There's only one possible safeguard to keep the proportions equal—work, work, the hardest work, the devil of a grind, gentlemen."

Dan gave a mirthless laugh. "Unless a man,

Mercedes 1104

his work, himself, are stronger than his temperament, then both of them are doomed. It's like a bark at sea with a cargo of precious stones on board, the ballast light. She's headed straight, she skims like a gull, the sails fill out. Then a sudden wind, a heavy sea, and over she goes— the cargo lost, the bark capsized. It happens that way to some of us, and it happened that way to Fabian."

Dan stopped in his walk suddenly. "You know the code of the sea, gentlemen? No captain who loses his ship should survive. He must stick to his bridge and go with it. Fabian, poor devil—his ancestors were Norsemen, the sea was in his blood. He had roamed and sailed all over the world, and he followed his traditions. When the shipwreck came he sank. Without a word, without a struggle, without an effort to save himself, as soon as his charts and compass were gone, his cargo lost, down he went!" A strange look flashed over Travis' face.

"Cowardly, my friends? No, don't say it, don't think it! I thought so myself long ago. But to watch another ship founder or to be on the ship yourself, your own ship, your own bridge giving way beneath you! There's a vital difference, I tell you! Whether by accident or misjudgment, recklessness or collision, for the fate of that

ship you're responsible. And to come back, to
face the world after that, alone, disgraced, empty-
handed, homeless, with nothing to live for, a past
full of memories and a future full of horror— why
a man must be mad, stark, raving mad! My God
my God! If he knew, if he dreamed what it
meant——"

Travis' voice broke. He stood there, breathing
heavily for a moment. His teeth were clenched,
he was pale as death, trying in vain to control
himself. Barry put out his hand and touched him.

"Yes, Whittemore—yes. All right, old man.
What's the matter? It was only this story of
Fabian's. I don't want you to blame him too
much. You don't know what you'd have done
yourself, if you had been in his place. Wait until you have heard the facts; then you'll understand perhaps what I meant, why—the reason
I envy him. Let me see, let me see! Where
was I?"

Pressing both hands to his forehead, he flung the
grasp of his friend aside, half angrily, impatiently,
striding off to the end of the studio.

"Oh, of course! I was just telling you, that
Perry had been such a traveller. The truth is,
the trouble began on his trip through the upper
Amazon, the winter before his marriage. He was
there with a German professor; the one for

science, the other for hunting, and they made common cause together. They combined to discover curari. You never heard of that, Doctor?"

Ménard, with his eyes on Travis' face, shook his head absent-mindedly.

"Well, very few have, I believe. It seems it's a vegetable poison, and the Indians use it to tip their hunting-arrows. A dead secret, gentlemen; worth its weight in gold to any one who can buy it, but the composition's a mystery. For a hundred years now scientists have been investigating, trying in vain to bribe, borrow, steal the plants from which the stuff is derived; but the Indians lie low. This professor, it seems, had been sent out by a German university to hunt down the curari for the sake of its medical properties; for that and for nothing else. He told Fabian all about it; and the two of them wandered for months there, in and out through the Indian villages, searching, spying, experimenting. Once they were actually present at the boiling of the witch's broth, a complicated ceremony with religious rites and dancing; but all to no purpose. The more they saw the less they knew. After a year of wandering, they were neither of them a jot wiser than they had been twelve months before.

Fabian didn't care. He'd been hunting big

The Bachelor Dinner

game and having a rousing time. Curari was nothing to him. But the professor, mindful of the university behind him and letters after his name, kept up his potterings day and night. The search began to look hopeless. Whether it was that, or sheer boredom, or letters from his fiancée in Italy, I don't know, but Perry resolved to quit. One last attempt and then back to civilization. The day was set, the return expedition formed. A small quantity of the curari in an Indian jar was all they had gained for their trouble. Still ignorant of its ingredients in spite of all their testings, they started back down the Amazon.

It was then, through one of the native guides, that they first got possession of the blow-gun; a real Indian blow-gun with a couple of the native arrows. The native prepared it before them. A curious scene that must have been, picturesque, extraordinary, as Perry used to recount it.

Just at sundown, in the heart of that vast wilderness, the two men and the black guide crouched in the shadow together; beyond, grazing, a great stag, solitary, unsuspicious, its antlers red with the dying rays, the forest all around them. In a flash the Indian snatched up one of the arrows, small, innocent-looking, like a penquill feathered with cotton. He tipped it with the curari, aimed the blow-gun, and fired. A

278

slight puff, scarcely audible above the rustling of the forest; and the animal, hearing nothing, feeling a prick in its flank, stopped grazing and looked around, evidently seeking instinctively for the insect that had stung it. The stag stared straight at the blow-gun, sniffing the air a little. After a moment the antlers drooped; it lowered its head as if sleepy. Seeing this, the Indian sprang forward, darting out of the shadow.

To the men's surprise, the stag still gazed fearlessly, as if curious; for all the world, as Perry said, like a sheep in a home pasture. It never moved a muscle; it stood there rigid, motionless. The Indian went nearer. Still no movement to run away. The breathing seemed perfectly natural. All at once the stag sank down. As it did so, the Indian approaching, laid his hand on the animal's shoulder. There was no start, no trembling, not a sign of resentment. It lay like a creature spellbound. The minutes passed. Every time it was touched, it would open its eyes, but its breath became shorter and slower. There was no blood, no wound, no sign where the arrow had struck it. Eighteen minutes in all by the watch, and the stag lay dead at their feet.

Now that, gentlemen, is the curari incident as Fabian told it to me. An odd story, but a true one. The professor died shortly after; and in

The Bachelor Dinner

Perry's own studio—I've seen it often myself—
in the midst of his collection of trophies, there
hung this identical blow-gun. The curari pot,
locked away in an inner drawer of his cabinet, was
often brought out and shown. Indeed in his
own house, at dinners, whenever hunting tales
were told, this was Fabian's favorite adventure.
Many a time around his table I've heard him tell
it to a roomful; tell it with various frills and addi-
tions according to his mood, but always ending
the same way, with a laugh, a lift of his wine-
glass.

"'Pon my word, gentlemen,' he would say, 'believe me or not as you choose; but there's the stag
head over yonder, there's the blow-gun with its
arrow, the only one left, and here's the curari!
Poison, deadliest poison, even a drop! Keep
away from the jar, please. 'Pon my word, on the
book— ha, ha, ha! Here's to the truth of it,
gentlemen!'

Among the guests who were often at Perry's
house was a lawyer, a young politician, a self-
made man, a rising man with whom he was very
friendly. Suddenly something happened. What
it was—whether the two collided in regard to the
same woman, as gossip had it, or not, I never
heard the details. At any rate all intercourse
ceased. Their relations snapped like——"

Mercedes 1104

Travis' gesture was graphic.

"There was something about that man," he said, "the look in his eye, his manner—somehow I always mistrusted him! It was early spring when the break occurred. A few weeks later, by the evening mail, I received a letter from Perry. The stamp was jammed on upsidedown, the envelope roughly sealed. Inside, these words blotted, illegible, scrawled on a half sheet: 'Dan, for God's sake, come to me! I'm in the devil of a——'

Then a huge blot and his name. The last word I couldn't make out. Was it fix, row, dilemma—what? Mechanically, still studying the blot, I took up the evening paper. There, in head-lines on the first page— To my dying day," said Travis, "I shall never forget that horror! The type, a foot high it seemed, swam up and down before me. 'Perry Fabian, the famous sculptor, well known in artistic and social circles, suspected of murdering his neighbor. The body of Van Roy, the banker, found dead in suspicious circumstances. No arrests made as yet. Startling developments expected.'

Underneath was a column, gentlemen, a whole column cleverly woven, full of innuendoes and slander, here and there a glint of the truth in between. This same truth so buried over with dirt,

The Bachelor Dinner

débris, moraine, like a glacier after an avalanche, that even I, his friend, aware of the infatuation, acquainted with most of the circumstances, having heard the tale from his own lips, and in spite of it, perhaps because of it, having faith in his ultimate honor— even I sat there open-mouthed, dumb-founded; too stunned to disentangle the real from the false, the truth from the lie! Van Roy— you understood, didn't you?—Van Roy was the woman's husband.

It was late the night before, they said, that Fabian left the house. He had been seen, so a witness told the coroner, hurrying down the banker's steps, distraught, bare-headed, in evening dress, with his right hand hidden behind him. In the morning the body was found, lying easily, naturally, as if asleep, stretched out on the divan. There was no wound, no bruise, nothing to indicate violence. On the floor to one side lay a quill pen; at least so they supposed. The coroner picked it up. At the first glance he was mystified. The quill was feathered with cotton.

It was then all the gossip of the place broke loose. Perry's story was recalled—the blow-gun, the stag, the curari—his late flight from the banker's house, the frequent meetings and the intimacy, not with Van Roy himself, but with his wife. The fact that that very evening the two had dined to-

Mercedes 1104

gether alone, while the banker was in the city, the latter returning suddenly, unexpectedly, unknown to the maids, letting himself in with his latch-key. And then the state of the woman herself, prostrated, hysterical, half crazy with grief or excitement, no one could tell which.

So it went on down the column. With every line, with every syllable, the net drew closer about my friend; he was caught in a thousand meshes! At the last word," said Travis, "I flung the paper from me, snatched up my hat and ran. The clocks were just striking midnight when, leaving the train at the pretty suburban station, hurrying across lots as fast as the absence of moon would permit, I entered the Fabian grounds.

Next door was the banker's house, deserted, lifeless, the shutters closed, the whole place dark as a tomb. Perry's light, to my relief, was burning over the front door. I followed its rays down the path. Was it a good omen or not? Were the police there on guard, or was he alone with his wife? As I hurried nearer, still speculating, watching the flicker for guidance, all of a sudden in front of the door I caught sight of the Mercedes; heard it even before I saw it. The big, scarlet touring car, its number 1104 gleaming out of the shadows, was puffing and panting like a live thing. A dark form bent over the motor. The

The Bachelor Dinner

front door, just ajar, let a rift of light through. To my astonishment I recognized Fabian. One leap over the grass plot and I had my hand on his shoulder. He jumped to his feet as if struck.

'Good Lord! You— you, Travis? I thought for a moment, I——'

Perry stood there staring at me. He was trembling like an aspen. Almost— it was odd, but it seemed to me as if he resented my coming. His friendship was on the defensive.

'Hello! What's the matter?'

'Matter?' he said slowly.

'Why, yes! You sent for me, didn't you? I had your letter and came straight on, took the first train; and here I am!'

'Oh, did I write?' said Perry. 'So I did. I forgot. Excuse me, old man; but when the blow first landed it knocked me all to pieces. I must have been out of my senses.' He bent down over the machine again, turning his shoulder toward me. 'Yes, yes, as I say, when a blow falls like that, when it strikes you straight between the eyes— So you saw the papers, did you?'

'Saw them—yes! A pack of lies and rubbish! Have you thought yet, have you decided what's to be done, Perry?'

'Done! Nothing.' He bent still lower. 'Not all lies or rubbish, as you ought to know, Dan;

Mercedes 1104

you better than any one. Hush! Speak lower!
My wife's in there behind that door. She hasn't
laid eyes on the papers. She doesn't know anything about it. She doesn't dream— my God,
not yet!'

Fabian, with a smothered cry, reached out for
the crank. He began to work it fiercely. His
face in the darkness looked haggard; his form
was bent like an old man's. The machine, re-
sponding as a horse to the spur, shook, shivered
under the pressure.

'A moment more,' he cried, 'and I'll be off!
The fact is, if you want to know, Dan, I am facing
a terrible question; and there's only the one answer. You ask what I've decided? I've racked
my brains in vain to solve it another way, but
there's only the one solution. Don't speak of
it, don't question me. I've got to act quickly
and I've got to act at once. Tomorrow would be
too late.' He flung a backward glance over his
shoulder.

'If the police should once walk through my
gate! That fellow, that former friend of mine, is
the prosecutor. Didn't you see it? He's responsible for those head-lines. He knows what you
do, Travis; and he's in this for revenge. He's
not the man to let the grass grow under his feet
for nothing. He's bound to strike, and soon. And

The Bachelor Dinner

when he strikes— God, Dannie! It's not myself
I'm thinking of, but that little woman inside there!
Her holy of holies dragged in the mud, her heart
trampled, besmirched, her faith, her ideals, her
illusions all smashed! You know what our court-
rooms are, Travis!

They'll snap and snarl like a pack of wolves
fighting over their carrion. The carrion may be
a poor thing enough; he may deserve what he
gets and more. But think of the woman who
loves him! Think of her, watching that scuffle,
watching every snap of those dripping jaws as
they tear and worry his heart out. If I could
only speak, Dan! If I could only speak out and
defend myself! But I can't; my tongue is tied.
Don't ask why, don't ask how. There are times
when a man may be guilty partly, innocent
mostly, and yet be unable to prove it. For his
honor's sake unable, or for the honor of some one
else.'

Fabian came closer. His voice as he spoke was
broken, strained. He stretched out his hand and
I clasped it.

'Don't misunderstand me, my friend. You
believe in me, yes; but no one else will, no one
else can. That arrow was out of my blow-gun!
I've got to go now, I've got to go, old fellow. But
first, just once, let me say one thing. I want you

to remember it afterward. In spite of all I may have done, in spite of all I told you, in spite of everything, I have loved my wife, I have cared for her, her alone through it all. I dare not tell her myself, I dare not open her eyes; but if anything should happen— She's in there, Dan, behind that door. Go in and comfort her, will you?'

Before the words were out of his mouth, the door swung back suddenly. His wife stood there on the threshold. The instant we laid eyes on her face, we were both sure that she knew. There was a look on it difficult to measure, impossible to describe; the look of one whose body and mind have gone through some deadly struggle, whose tears have all been shed, whose earthly ties have snapped. By a supreme effort of will the spirit, rising like a pure flame where the rest had crumbled to ashes, shone through the shell undaunted, triumphant, even ecstatic. The love in her face made me turn away. I drew back in the shadow," said Travis, "standing there motionless, holding my breath. There was something sacred about it.

When Fabian saw that look, the lever slipped from his grasp; he dropped his head in his hands with a groan. Whether he gave up his last hope then, whether he saw that it was too late, or whether her look compelled him, I don't know, gentlemen; nobody ever will know. With his

The Bachelor Dinner

teeth clenched and his face set, he lifted her into the car; then he leaped to her side and threw in the clutch. A moment of straining, shuddering, like a balky horse refusing to start, then the Mercedes swerved, turned with a roar. They shot out of sight into the darkness."

Travis hesitated a moment, wiping the sweat from his forehead.

"The rest— you remember, Barry? The rest was all in the papers. There's a famous drive in that region, dangerous by daylight for any machine, at night almost impossible. Ten miles along a sheer cliff with a drop from the road straight down, a hundred feet more or less. They call it the *Dead Man's Bend*. That night as it happened, strangely enough, a workman was coming along it. He heard a roar, felt a puff of wind, and jumped out of the way just in time. An automobile dashed past him; an automobile going, he said, at sixty miles an hour. On the seat were a man and a woman. The two were clinging together. That was all he could see as the car shot by. But the part that struck him as extraordinary—in spite of the speed, in spite of the precipice, there was no terror, no struggle, not a cry broke the stillness. They were lost, and they must have known it; no power on earth could save them. Yet— the workman swore to this on his oath— the faces of both were happy. The faces of both——"

Suddenly Travis' last words were lost in a crash of thunder so prolonged, so near, that we all started up. It was like a volley of heavy artillery. The branches, lashed by the wind, swayed and moaned. The rain began falling in torrents. At the first clap Ménard, being the nearest, dragged the curtains out of the wet, shut the windows down with a slam.

"An odd thing, that!" The Doctor looked around. "A storm in nature is like a storm in a human life. It's on you before you know it. A clap out of a cloudy sky! You may have been watching that very sky, you may have been following the thunder; yet before the windows of the soul can be closed, the rain has come pouring in, drowning, deluging——" He shook the drops from his coat-sleeves.

"Yes, Dannie, it's odd!" he said. "Mark me, I don't blame the man at all, if it was suicide, although I doubt it. He made a fatal mistake which circumstances, as it turned out, made impossible to redeem without injury to another; and his life was the reparation. But this to me is the stumbling-block. An automobile dashing over the cliffs— that has happened a score of times; it might just as well have been an acci-

The Bachelor Dinner

dent. But would a man let his own wife, or a woman her husband for that matter— Would any person who loved another— By heaven, Dan, what's the matter?"

Travis had stopped pacing; he was standing by the table motionless. In spite of the darkness, as the Doctor exclaimed, we could see that his whole form was rigid.

"What's the matter? Speak, Dan!"

"Hush!" said Travis. "Hush!... Didn't you hear something?"

He listened intently for a moment.

"Strange! No, I'm mistaken! I could have sworn— For a second there, it was just as if some one were sobbing. God, how that sound haunts me! Every day, every night! It's been going on now for years. In the midst of my work, in the midst of my sleep, I start up thinking I hear it."

As Travis said this, half stammering, he turned on the Doctor passionately.

"That— that question you were putting just now, Ménard! You could only have asked that from ignorance. You don't know—how should you without some hell-born knowledge—what it is for the one who is left! Left behind, left alone with remorse, despair, uncertainty; devils that cling to his footprints, mocking him with illu-

Mercedes 1104

sions, driving him mad with torture! Doctor, I
tell you this; and I know. Leave your enemy so,
if you must—the worst enemy that a man can
have. Even then the punishment would be worse
than the crime, the revenge would be more than
enough. But to leave any one that you care for
so, to live on with that curse! Doctor, better
strike him dead with your own hand, put a bullet
through his heart! It would be kinder in the end.
For my part, for my own part——"

Travis was breathing heavily.

"For years now it has been one long fight to
keep my brain clear, to keep my hand steady;
to keep in fact from my revolver over yonder.
One shot, one little shot! If it hadn't been for
this research work, these dangerous germ experiments——" Dan laughed out grimly.

"Why did I take it up, gentlemen? Why did
I stick to it? Why, up to date, hasn't it killed
me? Because I want to die, and I can't. Because, like Atlas, the weight of the world is too
heavy; I am bearing what is unbearable. And
I've borne it as long as I can, I've borne it as
long——"

As Travis said this, with his teeth set, his
hands clenched, suddenly into the smoke-filled
room shot a streak of vivid lightning—sharp,
jagged, zigzag, baring for a second every object

291

The Bachelor Dinner

there, cutting through the air like a rapier. A flash, and then it was gone! But in that flash— not a soul who was in that room that night to their death-bed will ever forget it. As the bright streak lit up the gallery, the spiral stair and the doorway, it disclosed the form of a woman; slight, pale, staring down, leaning against the panels, her hands clasped, her eyes full of tears. She was trembling, breathless, quivering like a leaf. Her whole soul was centred on Travis.

The flash seemed an eternity. We all sat motionless, petrified.

It was then, as the lightning went out like a torch, Dan gave a great leap through the darkness. A cry burst from his throat, followed by another cry like an echo. Hidden by the darkness, shrouded by the smoke, the two met on the gallery. A moment of paralyzed silence; then with mutual instinct we sprang to our feet.

"Gentlemen," said Ménard in a whisper, "Come! My experiment is over; it has been successful. I invite you all to my rooms next door, to drink to our host, to drink to his wife. A happy ending to the Bachelor Dinner!"